Crossing the Lines

Books by Sulari Gentill

The Rowland Sinclair Series
A Few Right Thinking Men
A Decline in Prophets
Miles off Course
Paving the New Road
Gentlemen Formerly Dressed
A Murder Unmentioned
Give the Devil His Due

The Hero Trilogy
Chasing Odysseus
Trying War
The Blood of Wolves

Other Novels
Crossing the Lines

Crossing the Lines

Sulari Gentill

Poisoned Pen Press

Library of Congress Catalog Card Number: 2017934125

ISBN: 9781464209147   Hardcover
       9781464209161   Trade Paperback

This is an original work in its entirety by Sulari Gentill

Poisoned Pen Press
4014 N. Goldwater Blvd., Suite 201
Scottsdale, AZ 85251
www.poisonedpenpress.com
info@poisonedpenpress.com

Printed in the United States of America

Prologue

When the man was murdered, the gallery was full of voyeurs. They'd come to see and be seen, to admire and be admired. In their finery they'd postured and praised the artist, considering each canvas, looking carefully at every mark of the brush, discerning nuance and tone and meaning. They eyed each other as rivals in fashion and wit, in the sycophantic ability to recognise artistic genius. The show belonged to art and artists and art lovers. And so no one noticed the writer.

When the body was discovered, there were screams of horror. Some sobbed on seeing the corpse; others could barely contain their glee. The gallery staff soothed and apologised, management called insurers, the authorities barked orders and asked questions. They listened for guilt, for motive and lies. And no one heard the writer.

When the dead man was identified, many claimed intimacy. Some had worked with him, others had danced in his arms. Several people purported friendship, a few admitted to a mutual loathing. They offered opinions and insights, analyses of character. And yet no one knew the writer.

On Introductions

What if you wrote of someone writing of you?
In the end, which of you would be real?

IN THE BEGINNING she was a thought so unformed that he was aware only of something which once was not.

And there was the idea. The embryonic notions of story. Fragile swirling mists that struggled to find patterns; sense that was made and unmade and made yet again. In time there were shapes in the clouds and there was her.

They were shy with each other at first. Stiff.

It took the longest time to exchange names. Many were considered and discarded until, finally, one was familiar. One rang true.

She wrote books—quirky whimsical mysteries with an eye for the absurd. Her pen was light and her voice assured. Even so, she had not been born with the knowledge that she would write, but happened upon storytelling accidentally while seeking some unknown distraction. In writing she found meaning and purpose and a kind of spiritual joy. And like many who come late to religion, her devotion to the craft was absolute, her conviction in its power unshakeable.

Yet she hesitated before calling herself a writer lest it seem presumptuous, or affected, or just plain silly. Some small part of her recoiled from claiming her place aloud too absolutely.

Her work had achieved a modicum of success, though she was by no means a household name.

He called her Madeleine d'Leon. Her husband would call her Maddie.

She was thirty and—when they first came to know of one another—happy.

Madeleine was a lawyer...she'd been a lawyer first. She practised in the corporate sector, but she didn't like to talk of work or even think about work when her time was her own.

"My concern is billable," she'd proclaim when asked about some matter she'd left at the office. "If I'm not being paid, I just don't care."

But she'd married a man who cared all the time. Hugh Lamond was the doctor. Not just a doctor, but *the* doctor. Ashwood was not large enough or gentrified enough to have more than "the doctor" and Hugh Lamond was it. Every man, woman, and child in Ashwood knew who he was and assumed he cared about each small twinge or ache or concern, regardless of whether it was his anniversary or his wife's birthday. They were right.

In the beginning Madeleine had thought it funny: the god-like status of the country doctor. And Hugh was after all charming and committed. If anyone deserved to be a small-town god, it was him. Now it niggled just a little that she had been lost in his divine glory, a handmaiden to his social deity. But still, she was proud of him.

So Madeleine worked, commuting when she had to and advising from home when she could. In her non-billable hours she painted, and sewed and built a garden which would grow to be worthy of the grand home they would have…when they got round to renovating.

And then one day, whilst sitting in a particularly tedious meeting on some technical matter for which a lawyer's presence was merely decorative, Madeleine d'Leon had an idea for a story, and the very first thought of him.

The moment of genesis was strong, a cell of creativity that divided and multiplied until there was life. He had barely any substance at all…just a space in the narrative for a protagonist of some sort.

She began writing then and there, raising her head occasionally to nod so her colleagues would think she was taking notes about the meeting itself. Every now and then she would arch a brow and shake her head or rub her chin while frowning, or tap the table with her lips pressed tightly together. She called it her boardroom technique…the kind of lawyerly intimations of consideration that made people feel better regardless. It was Madeleine's conviction that her clients demanded the presence of their lawyers at these meetings, not because they needed them, or even planned to listen to them, but because the legal profession was a kind of security blanket. She was paid for what she called corporate hand-holding and the nature of Madeleine was such that she was not too proud to admit it.

In that meeting she discovered just one thing about him, but oh, what a thing! What a perfect link! He was a writer. It was their connection. He would see the world as she did: in stories, or potential stories, in vignettes and themes. He would judge people as characters, each with their own story. They would look upon his world together.

She called him Edward McGinnity. His friends would call him Ned.

He was twenty-eight when she found him, a young man with the world at his feet and no idea of how he should step into it.

Edward McGinnity had always known he would write. It was as natural to him as breathing and he suspected the consequences of stopping would be as dire. In his mind there had always been epics, tales which carried on the books he could not bear to end, and new stories with conglomerate characters and modified plots. Eventually he'd picked up a pen.

At first he'd written poetry, as adolescents do. Learned to weave words with angst and defiance and heartbreak. Those old verses embarrassed him now, melodramatic, flowery, pretentious, but every so often there was one line, one phrase which was clear and strong and perfect. As he grew into a man, Edward McGinnity learned to pull back, to leave the louder things unsaid, to call out to the whispers once drowned in waves of passionate literary excess. And he found new stories and a desire to be read.

Maintained by an inheritance, an income born of tragedy, Edward lived well. He did so quietly, aware that the ability to write unencumbered from the first was too enviable to be broadcast, too likely to invite failure as a karmic balancing of luck.

He was sitting on his deck, with a notebook and a glass of red when her story first struck him. He knocked over the glass in his haste to grab the pen beside it, allowing the wine to soak and stain the decking timbers as he tried to pin the thought onto his page with ink. In time he stood and paced as he wrote, stopping occasionally to laugh, so giddy was he with the discovery of her. He knew she was a writer before he knew her name.

• • ● • •

Madeleine called Hugh that evening, as she did every evening that work took her away. The custom was more utilitarian than romantic—should she pick up milk in Ashwood?—that sort of thing. But this night she was exhilarated and she loved Hugh Lamond more for the fact that she could share it with him. She knew she was babbling but the idea was powerful now. It pulled new ideas towards it, building a world of characters and themes and events around itself. Hugh seemed a little bewildered at first but perhaps whatever it was that possessed Madeleine was infectious, for soon he had suggestions and thoughts. She told him about Edward McGinnity, her well-heeled writer.

"But this is going to be a murder mystery, isn't it?" Hugh asked.

"Yes."

"So he's a crime-writer?"

"No. Edward writes literary novels…the kind of worthy incomprehensible stuff that wins awards." Madeleine paced with the phone, unable to physically contain her excitement. "That's the irony, you see. The hero of my crime fiction wouldn't lower himself to read, let alone write the stuff himself. He's a serious artist."

"But if he was a crime-writer he'd know what to do to solve the crime."

"That's too predictable, Hugh. The fact that he is so out of place in a crime fiction will make it interesting."

"Fair enough. Perhaps his family shouldn't approve of his writing?" Hugh ventured.

Madeleine smiled, touched that he was so interested. "But why wouldn't they approve?"

"They might want him to be a doctor. You know, there aren't enough books about doctors."

Madeleine laughed. "No, I think his family is dead," she said. "An accident of some sort…the story will work better if he's alone in the world."

"Why?"

"I don't know…there's something alluring about the lonely hero."

"He can't be too lonely. He'll need a love interest of some sort."

"Why?"

"Because he's a man…it's what we do."

Madeleine groaned. "If he has a love interest, I'll have to write a sex scene."

"Well that's to be avoided at all costs," Hugh agreed. "She could be dead too—the love interest, I mean," he said helpfully. "He could be a grieving husband."

"Maybe…" Madeleine considered the idea. The death of Edward McGinnity's family was probably grief enough. She didn't want her hero to be completely withdrawn and bitter. "What if he loves someone who doesn't love him back, but who might one day?" she said. "That way I won't have to write a sex scene because she won't have him. Perhaps Edward is so in love with her that he can't move on."

"Won't that make him look pathetic?"

"It'll make him look deep."

"I don't know, I'm thinking pathetic."

"If I hadn't married you, you would have pined forever."

"Hmmm…yes…forever. Or at least a week. What time will you get home?"

"Should be back before lunch tomorrow."

"Grab some milk on the way in, will you?"

• • ● • •

Madeleine spent the evening in the familiar, generic solitude of a hotel room. She discarded her board papers onto the small table by the window and heaved her bag onto one of the twin beds. Changing into pyjamas, she ordered room service and settled into the other bed to open her laptop.

The novel would begin with him…it had to. That was how crime fiction worked—subplots, clues, red herrings all channelled through a single literary device: the protagonist. The reader would have to know him and trust him for the story to work. So she would open with him, and worry about the murder later.

Madeleine closed her eyes. She could see him: sitting on the open deck of his expensive beach house, oblivious to the ocean view as he worked on the great Australian novel. She smiled. Of course he would write longhand, every word chosen after consideration, deliberation, and requisite suffering. The man she saw was handsome. For a moment she wondered when she'd decided that. His hair was dark, blown wild by the salt breeze against which his collar was turned up. The sky and the sea were both grey and turbulent. And yet he continued to write, muttering to himself as he tapped the pen against his chin. It was not until the first fat drops fell that he seemed to notice. Cursing, he closed his notebook against the rain and stepped through the French doors into the house.

The house itself would be tastefully furnished. Modern designer pieces complemented by what might be called sentimental junk. A large basin made of kilned glass was filled with old matchbox cars in anything but collectible condition. An assortment of old cameras, Box Brownies, Vollendas, leather-cased Kodaks, took up several bookshelves. A professional quality digital SLR sat on the kitchen bench beside the wine rack.

There was no dust…because, of course, he would have a housekeeper. A quietly spoken, motherly woman called Mrs. Jesmond. Madeleine paused, pleased by the detail. Jill Jesmond had worked with her at Morrison McArthur. She was anything but quietly spoken but she'd love being in Edward's story, even as his housekeeper.

There were several picture frames on the sideboard—an eclectic collection of the kind of beautiful frames bought as particular gifts: silver, etched glass, tooled leather. Only one contained a picture, a family photo from the decade before. That must have been his family—parents, brother, little sister—all now gone. Madeleine lingered over that photo…the anguish of losing everybody at once, the loneliness of it. The rest of the frames were empty, blank. He was a man…perhaps he had just not got around to filling them…perhaps it was something else.

The rain was heavy now. It curtained off the world around the house with a fall of water, blurring everything without. Edward checked his watch and cursed. It was a gentle, old-fashioned way of cursing that reminded Madeleine of her grandfather. Words not even considered swearing in this age. It was interesting, given the sleek modernity of the décor.

He ran up the iron staircase to the bedrooms on the floor above. Edward McGinnity's bedroom was neat, no random deposits of clothes, the bed made and taut, a dozen or so notebooks of various style and size were stacked in an orderly tower on the upended trunk beside his bed. It was a masculine room, functional and unadorned except for one painting. A nude in oil in an Art Deco frame. The composition was simple and the pose direct. The brushwork evoked a certain wistfulness. Somehow Madeleine knew the artist had loved his model…it was perfect.

Edward stripped as he walked into the en suite to shower. The water did little to soothe the tension from his body. Every muscle was tight, wound, ready to begin. He loved this part. Discovery yawned before him and it was glorious. The sheer possibility, exhilarating beyond measure. How seductive the existential strain between writer and character—almost erotic. Edward was charged with the liminal intimacy of it. Not only would he know her, she would come to know him. And therein would be the danger and the essence of story.

She'd be a crime-writer. Edward smiled. He'd always considered authors of detective fiction an interesting breed. They identified with their genre more than other novelists, inhabiting a definite subculture in the literary world. There was a naivety about crime-writers that intrigued him…an underlying belief in heroes and justice, despite the darkness of their work. And sometimes, just sometimes, a crime-writer would be accepted into the literary elite, lauded for style, despite a dogged commitment to plot and pace. It would allow him to test her sense of literary self, as he intended.

Madeleine d'Leon would begin as a vignette of middle-class success. Professionally and personally contented. A lawyer, with a lawyer's detachment and dedication to reason, she would live in the country in fulfilment of the bourgeoisie yearning for views of trees and cows. But there was an honesty about Madeleine d'Leon, a humour that recognised absurdity. Hers was a mind he wanted to know, hers was a life suited to prose.

He'd been searching for her all afternoon. In the beginning she had been elusive, soft, but she was clear now. Small, not conventionally beautifully but with a smile that made her so. She possessed the kind of face that seemed always to be thinking. She laughed sometimes for no outwardly discernible reason, but because something in the perpetual movement of her mind had amused her.

Edward dressed quickly, knowing he was late. Shirt, cuff links, watch, bow tie, dinner suit. He checked his breast pocket for the invitation, stopping to glance at the naked woman on his wall. He'd purchased her in a small gallery just out of Paris, and she had owned him since then. His muse. Edward thanked her for Madeleine d'Leon.

Murder Amongst Other Things

Madeleine thought about the murder all the way back to Ashwood. It was a three-hour drive. The roads were familiar and required just enough attention to allow her to think, but not too hard.

Someone would have to die, that went without saying. It would have to be someone who mattered to Edward McGinnity. Unlike their police procedural counterparts, amateur detectives needed a reason to investigate.

Madeleine watched as the scene unfolded before her. The gallery was crowded with the exquisitely elegant. Thin, svelte women who glittered discreetly, whose eyes longingly followed the waiters with their silver trays of hors d'oeuvres. And men who seemed, well, less hungry. A lone cellist provided a tasteful backing to cultured conversations. Edward stood by himself with a glass of champagne, gazing somewhat distantly at one of the large modernist works on display. He looked comfortable in his dinner suit, standing naturally without the need to finger his collar or adjust incessantly. He had a good tailor, perhaps…probably. Or he wore a dinner suit often.

Madeleine sighed. Men looked so handsome in formal attire. Hugh hadn't worn his dinner suit since they were married. She wondered if it still fitted him.

A young woman approached Edward McGinnity and he smiled in a way that made Madeleine's breath catch. So this was she: the woman who would be Edward's unrequited love. She was indeed a vision. A brunette, of course—the beautiful blonde was too cliché—soft and curved, her face was lit with an inherent mischief and an open warmth. She hugged Edward. A real hug, a genuine press, rather than some social affectation.

"Ned, I'm so glad you're here. I have no idea what these people are saying!"

Edward laughed—an easy laugh, but not loud. More an extension of his smile than an expression on its own. He left his arm around her shoulders—companionable rather than possessive. "But they're your paintings, Will," he whispered.

She took his glass and swigged the imported champagne. Her movements were graceful, imbued with a natural theatre. "Yes, but they're *interpreting* them… with words I don't understand so I don't know what I'm pretending to have painted!" She grabbed his lapel. "You have to stay with me…these are your people… you understand their strange gibberish."

Madeleine slowed her car to a stop outside Ashwood's grocery shop. No wonder Edward loved her—she was fabulous! But why didn't she love him? Perhaps there was someone else.

"I am at your service, Ms. Meriwether," Edward said, bowing his head.

The young artist shoved him gently. "I'm serious. Don't leave me...not for a moment."

"So Elliot isn't with you tonight?"

She shook her head, her brow creased just slightly. "No, he hates this sort of thing. He won't even go to his own openings."

Edward said nothing. Elliot Kaufman was a selfish bastard, but Willow loved him.

She entwined her arm in his. "Shall we mingle?"

Madeleine contemplated the scenario. The corpse would have to, of itself, drag Edward McGinnity into an investigation. It would have to be someone he cared about or perhaps someone he might have reason to kill himself—the clear-my-name motive. She already liked Willow Meriwether too much to take the former route. It would have to be the latter. Perhaps Elliot Kaufman... but that would leave Willow unspoken for. No...too much depended on Edward's love being unrequited.

Who else would a novelist kill? And then the answer came, in a sharp spreading burst of realisation. Of course.

"Oh, no." Willow tightened her grasp on Edward's arm. "Don't look now."

Edward swore, the same quaint old-world form of cursing that Madeleine had heard before.

The man who approached them wore a kind of stylistic uniform that badged him as a man of letters and of means. A flamboyance that was both unique and standard. A screen-printed silk scarf draped around his shoulders like a shawl and his bow tie sat askew. A burgundy felt fedora was set on his head at a studiously jaunty angle. He kissed everybody he met, man and woman, with loud exclamations of delight and a three-kiss ritual that didn't involve any actual contact.

"He's seen us, it's too late," Willow murmured. "Courage, dear one, we'll face him together. Try not to be rude."

"Neddie, Willow…how are you my darlings?" Geoffrey Vogel advanced upon them with his arms outstretched as though he was accepting applause. "My congratulations, beautiful lady," he said kissing Willow. "Don't think I didn't notice your little tribute to *moi*." He pressed his palms together and bowed. "I am very touched and humbled."

"Really? Which piece was that?" Edward directed the question at Vogel as he doubted Willow would have the slightest clue.

Vogel pointed to a painting near the fire exit. It depicted a desk by an open window. The desk was untidy, strewn with handwritten notes and crumpled pages. A yellow-faced honeyeater had, it seemed, flown in through the window to perch on a pen. It was Edward's desk, in fact. Willow had refused to let him continue working until she'd made the sketches she'd needed. The bird had been a bonus attracted by the half-eaten honey sandwich left on top of a stack of notebooks. The use of light and shadow was characteristic of Willow Meriwether's work. It gave what was essentially a still life a life that was anything but still. She called the piece *Literatum scripius excellio*. It wasn't Latin; just some Harry Potter-inspired abomination that the artist had come up with after too much wine.

"Of course *vogel* is the German word for bird," Vogel explained with a nod at Willow. "See how the dear little chap perches upon the pen, controlling the excesses and the folly of the writer. Notice that the light falls to create an illumination which transforms the creature into a guiding light, towards which all the other writing instruments are pointed. Of course I recognised the writing on these pages...that of a certain Mr. Edward McGinnity, whose debut novel I had the privilege of editing into shape." Vogel raised his brows and nudged Edward. "This delightful, insightful masterpiece is a very touching homage to my modest role. A wonderfully subtle work...quite breathtaking in its depth. As I said Willow, darling, I am very humbled, but the tribute is, I assure you, unnecessary."

Edward drained his glass of champagne and looked for another.

"Do tell me about your latest project, Neddie. I understand that first novel we worked on together hasn't yet been published. Pity. I thought I'd done enough, but obviously not."

Willow groaned audibly.

"I pulled it, not the publisher." Edward decided that there was no reason to keep the peace. No reason that was good enough, anyway. "I wouldn't put my name to that penny dreadful into which you turned my novel."

"Ned," Willow cautioned.

Vogel's lips curved up in a facsimile of cordiality, but they were white and pressed tightly together. "I under-stand. The editing process is brutal...not all writers survive it. So what are you doing now, Neddie?"

Edward said nothing. Even if he was ready to share Madeleine with anyone, it would not be Vogel. The ruins of his first novel still smouldered bitterly—the characters, trapped in a manuscript defiled, haunted him. He'd abandoned them too easily, allowed Vogel to critique and strip and suggest them into silence. How he hated the man for that murder.

Madeleine nodded as she watched. She hated Vogel, too. Killing him would be a pleasure.

Vogel began a speech. Edward leaned over to kiss Willow's cheek and walked away.

• ● ● ● •

He spent the next hour moodily studying the exhibition, eating from the circulating silver platters of canapés and eavesdropping as the artistic community considered and judged the works of the audacious newcomer. Edward listened, amused, as each painting was reimagined and approved. He was happy for Willow. She would not be offended that they thought her painting of the neighbour's dog was an "exploration of self-doubt and melancholy." She wouldn't care as long as they bought enough to allow her to keep painting.

"That's the difference between your trade and mine— you need your readers to complete what you do," she would say as he struggled to smooth each sentence so the words would swirl about the tongue like water. "I would still paint if the world was dark and nobody could see anything."

When the artist found him again, he was musing on her words and his, with a miniature *vol-au-vent* in each hand.

"Give me one of those," Willow demanded. "I can't believe you left me!"

"Sorry, Will…I didn't want to cause a scene. Were you stuck with the pretentious, talentless, useless git?"

Willow shook her head. "He left soon after you did. I've been stuck with people from the gallery." She stood back and spun triumphantly, her cheeks flushed. "Apparently, I'm a sensation!"

Edward smiled. "But of course."

"There'll be speeches soon," she said a little distractedly.

He nodded. "It's only fitting that your life as a struggling artist be eulogised. Who's doing the honours?"

"The gallery director, Paulo Cotton. And I'll have to say something I suppose?"

"I expect you will." Edward was surprised she seemed so nervous. Willow Meriwether was born to lead revolutions. Addressing the masses was not something that had ever before concerned her. She pressed against him and he placed his arm about her shoulders and pulled her close.

"You'll be fine," he whispered. "They'll adore you as much as they do your work."

Willow sighed. "I can't think of a single art-related joke to open with."

"I wouldn't advise a joke—this is a very serious crowd. I'm not sure laughing is allowed…Hang on…" Edward rocked forward onto his toes. "What's going on over there?"

The commotion was restrained, dampened by gallery officials who flocked towards the fire exit.

Willow grabbed Edward's hand and pulled him towards the disturbance. "Let's find out!" Her eyes shone. "Perhaps it's a protestor!"

As ludicrous as the supposition was, Edward found himself unable to refuse her.

They manoeuvred through the crowd until it seemed too dense and resistant. The police had arrived now and were pushing the guests back.

"You have to let me through...I'm the artist!" Willow cried suddenly.

For a moment, everyone stopped, startled and confused. Willow moved quickly, sidestepping onto the landing of the stairwell and dragging Edward with her. They were jostled out again almost immediately, of course, but not before they'd seen the broken body of Geoffrey Vogel, his eyes wide and frozen. The editor's limbs were crumpled beneath him at strange jagged angles and his head was peculiarly offset from his neck.

Questions

Edward waited as the police questioned Willow. It has been three hours now since Vogel's body had been discovered. Nobody had been allowed to leave as the police gathered evidence, and questioned every person in turn. He was glad he'd been there for Willow...it was a terrible way for her exhibition to end, the triumph of her work eclipsed completely by a lurid sensation, the demise of a bloated fool. Edward did not mourn for Geoffrey Vogel.

He yawned. It was two in the morning and he hadn't yet had his turn in the office now being used as an interview room. Fleetingly, he wondered what his Madeleine would think of this...his protagonist was a crime-writer, after all. The death of Vogel was probably the stuff of plot and dreams.

He could see her behind the wheel of that old Mercedes she drove, her eyes bright, her lips twitching occasionally into furtive smiles as the story came to her.

She pulled into the drive. Smoke wafted out of the chimney—like a flag announcing that Hugh was at home. She turned off the engine, eager to tell him, to talk about the murder in her mind.

The air was cold and clouded with her breath. The morning fog lingered, shrouding the weatherboard house and the pebbled drive with its overhanging holly oaks, into a painterly softness.

Hugh came out to greet her. "Did you let the car cool down before you turned it off?"

"Yes," she lied.

"You should give it a couple of minutes after a long trip, Maddie," he said, sternly.

"Of course," she replied, kissing him. "You're the only man I know who can backseat-drive without being in the car."

"All of us *can* do it, but very few have the commitment, darling." He took her suitcase from the boot. "Jeeves made dinner—you're just in time."

Edward inhaled sharply, surprised by what he'd just done. His own father had always referred to take-away as "Jeeves," personifying convenience as a gentleman's valet. Jeeves was also what Gerard McGinnity had called the carwash, the pizza delivery-man, and the remote control. Edward wasn't sure why exactly he'd placed that memory into Hugh Lamond's mouth, but he didn't try to take it back.

"Did Jeeves cook fish and chips or Chinese food?" Madeleine followed her husband into the house.

Within, the home of Hugh Lamond and Madeleine d'Leon was comfortable, stylishly cluttered with whimsical pieces. The furniture was of an age that was more vintage than antique. The bookshelves were full, volumes stuffed horizontally in the gaps above the vertical spines. The walls held a tumultuous collection of paintings hung erratically but in somehow pleasing congregations.

Landscapes were grouped with life drawings and portraits, oils, pastels, and watercolours, even collage.

Madeleine dropped her satchel on the club armchair
closest to the door, slipped off her shoes and padded
barefoot into the bedroom. The bed was roughly made,
a hasty drawing up of the eiderdown over the lumps
beneath. Madeleine pulled back the covers and extracted
a set of striped flannelette pyjamas from under the
pillow.

Hugh brought in her bag and she disappeared into
the bathroom to change.

Edward's brow rose. It seemed a little odd to be so
coy with one's spouse, but it was charming in a way.
And strangely seductive.

Madeleine emerged in pyjamas already talking about
her book, elation causing the words to tumble with
neither pause nor breath.

Hugh listened, following her to the kitchen and
laying out plates and cutlery on the small wooden table.
He plonked a parcel into the table's centre, unwrapping
the butcher's paper to present a still-steaming meal of
battered fish and fat chips. He helped himself. "Jeeves
has outdone himself this time," he said gazing happily
at his overflowing plate. "Remind me to give him the
afternoon off next Sunday."

Madeleine reached over and took a chip from his plate,
though there were plenty left on the butcher's paper.

"So…what do you think?"

"About what?"

"About the story."

"I still think he should be a doctor. People love medical detectives."

Madeleine rolled her eyes. "Name one."

"Dr. Watson."

"He was the sidekick!"

"I suppose that's one way to read it."

"You're an idiot."

He chuckled. "Honestly, darling, it sounds great, but my opinion doesn't count."

"It counts." Madeleine reached for another chip.

"Leith called, by the way." Hugh left the table to switch the kettle on. "She wants you to have lunch with her tomorrow. Perhaps you should pass the idea by her?"

Again Edward was surprised by the subconscious juxtaposition of reality. Leith Henry was his own literary agent and one of his oldest friends. He trusted her with almost everything, including his work. She had supported his decision to pull from publication the novel Vogel had edited into ruin, commiserated with him and inspired him anew. She knew his writing and believed in it. Her advice was sharp and insightful but gently delivered in a manner that did not incite defence. Madeleine would need someone like Leith Henry...why should she not have the original?

He nodded slowly, pleased with the notion of anchoring her world to his, through his agent.

"How was your day?" Madeleine realised suddenly that they had not yet talked of Hugh at all.

"A nightmare, actually. I've had Mrs. Oswald to see me in tears."

"Because of Joe?" Madeleine was aware that Joe Oswald had suffered a massive stroke two weeks before. He'd survived but it seemed he was unlikely to ever recover.

"Sort of. The old bugger had everything in his name, apparently. The poor woman can't access anything. Joe's not dead so the will doesn't help."

"She doesn't have his power of attorney?"

Hugh smiled. "For a moment you sounded like a lawyer. No—Joe is only fifty-two—they didn't expect him to have a stroke.

"Nobody ever does. It's why everybody should have reciprocal powers of attorney in place."

"Do we?"

Madeleine squirmed. "No, we don't. I should be the one to take care of that, I suppose."

Hugh grimaced. "If something happened to me, you'd need to be able to make decisions about the surgery….Pay people, insurers, hire, fire…"

"Maybe we should have a proper lawyer draw up the documents, someone who specialises in that sort of thing," Madeleine suggested, a little alarmed by the prospect of dealing with the ins and outs of the surgery.

"Is that your way of getting out of it?"

"Yes."

"Mr. McGinnity, we're ready for you, sir."

The young policeman summoned him into the interview room just as Willow Meriwether came out. Edward grabbed her hand as they passed. "Are you all right, Will?"

She nodded. "I'll wait for you," she whispered.

He kissed her hand. "No, go home. It's late and Elliot will be worried."

She shook her head. "I'll wait."

"Mr. McGinnity," the policeman said again.

Edward went in.

The office was furnished with a desk and a meeting table, at which sat a bloody-eyed detective and a wide-eyed constable. The melamine surface of the table was clear except for a couple of coffee mugs and beige rings where the mugs had been previously placed.

The detective introduced himself as Bourke and invited Edward to take a seat. The constable said nothing. Apparently he was just there to take notes.

Edward gave his statement, such as it was. Name. Address. Yes, he knew the deceased, Geoffrey Vogel. No, he wouldn't say they were friends; they'd had a professional relationship once. Yes, he'd spoken to the deceased that night. He couldn't say where exactly he'd been when Vogel was killed because he was unsure when exactly that was, but he was somewhere in the gallery, possibly quite close to a tray of hors d'oeuvres.

Detective Bourke pushed hard on Edward's conversation with Vogel, extracting an almost verbatim account of what was said.

"Detective," Edward said in the end, "am I to understand that you don't believe Geoffrey Vogel's death was an accident?"

"Why do you say it was an accident?"

"I don't say anything. I just assumed he fell down the stairs…he'd been drinking…why don't you think it was an accident?"

Bourke answered cautiously. "We have reason to believe he may have been pushed."

"What reason?"

"By your own admission, Mr. McGinnity, you resented his interference with your work."

"He edited a novel badly. Vogel was a hack and a pompous fool, but that's hardly motive to push him down the fire stairs."

For a moment, Bourke studied him silently. Edward waited.

"What exactly is the nature of your relationship with Ms. Meriwether, Mr. McGinnity?"

"She's a friend."

"And what was Ms. Meriwether's relationship with the deceased?"

"Didn't you ask her?"

"Answer the question, Mr. McGinnity."

Edward shrugged. "I don't know. I think he was a fan of her work...beyond that I doubt they had a relationship."

Bourke snapped shut his notebook. "Thank you, Mr. McGinnity. We'll be in touch."

Edward stood, a little unsettled by the abrupt closure of the interview.

Bourke yawned.

Edward glanced at his watch. It was twenty past three. Perhaps the detective was just tired. God knows he was.

• ● ● ● •

Madeleine pulled the rug more tightly around her as she waited for Hugh to bring in coffee. It was one of those chilly evenings which came upon a sunny day and caught you by surprise. They hadn't yet organised that season's firewood nor started lighting the fires, and the house was cold.

Shivering, Madeleine rubbed her arms as Edward placed his jacket over Willow's shoulders, his hand on the small of her back as they emerged from the glassed entrance of the gallery. There were still clustered gatherings standing in the foyer and on the steps. A kind of sombre excitement prevailed and many glances were cast towards the artist whose debut in the national gallery had ended so dramatically.

"Willow, thank goodness I caught you!" Adrian Barrington jogged up to them with movements exaggerated to emphasise that he was not pleased with having to move so rapidly. He was a large man, as flamboyantly dressed as Geoffrey Vogel had been, but in a manner that seemed less slavishly engineered. There was an eccentric dignity about Barrington that Vogel had failed to achieve. He was Willow Meriwether's agent, a gourmet, a connoisseur of art and food and all things fine.

Madeleine liked him immediately.

He kissed Willow on both cheeks. "Congratulations, my darling…you've sold out. There was a bidding war on *Literatum scripius excellio*. Dear lady, you are officially a phenomenon!"

"Really?" Willow looked shocked. "I thought that after Geoffrey—"

"Well, that's the thing, my dear," Barrington shrugged. "The accident stalled demand, but once the rumours of murder got round, it was like the post-Christmas sales at Harrods. I had to beat them off! Who ever thought that overdressed philistine would make such a valuable contribution to the world of art!"

"Oh," Willow replied hesitantly.

"Darling, this is good news!" Barrington declared. "People will be talking about the Meriwether exhibition for years. Macabre provenance is highly bankable. Your career is made, my love!"

Edward put his arm around Willow and kissed the top of her head. "Not to mention that you are ludicrously talented."

"Of course, that too!" Barrington added hastily. "This incident just provides a little extra intrigue, applies a subtle nudge to those who have the exquisite taste to be considering a purchase of one of your pieces."

Willow sighed. "I'm not sure you could call a murder subtle, Adrian."

"Rubbish…it was the most subtle thing Geoffrey Vogel ever did!" He glanced at his watch. "I must go… James—pitiless bully that he is—has decreed a six-thirty start!"

"Can't you cancel? Surely he'd understand…."

"Understand?" Barrington said bitterly. "James' compassion is inversely proportional to the size of his biceps. His understanding was long ago bench-pressed into oblivion!" The art dealer's shoulders slumped despondently. "He will take one look at me and know I've had champagne and oysters…and those excellent little hamburgers on a stick, not to mention the salmon roulade and truffled cheese balls….He has some kind of sixth sense, I think—he can smell satiation, happiness, the consumption of anything other than celery in the last week. Oh, how I loathe the man!"

Edward tried not to smile. Adrian Barrington had a complicated relationship with his personal trainer. He paid the much-vilified James exorbitant sums to supervise his training regime and diet, and then did everything he could to thwart the man in his duty. It was a strangely subversive, masochistic ritual.

Barrington kissed Willow good-bye. "Think of me as you have your morning croissant, my love. I shall be in purgatory, paying for my trespasses with all the other tracksuit-clad sinners." He shook Edward's hand. "You'll see her home, won't you, Ned? After all, there's talk of a murderer on the loose!"

On Choices

Edward McGinnity and Willow Meriwether walked in silence to his car. He'd been forced to park the Mark II Jaguar over a kilometre away.

Madeleine took the mug of coffee Hugh offered her, wondering if she should mention that her protagonist was driving a Jaguar. She decided against it. Hugh could be a little irrational when it came to Jaguars.

"I'm starving," Willow confessed as Edward held the front passenger door open. "Every time I got anywhere near an hors d'oeuvre tray, some art nut wanted to talk to me."

"I'm not sure anything will be open at this time." He frowned as he considered the problem. Willow and Elliot were both artists…there would probably be nothing resembling food in their terrace. "We could stop in at my place and raid the fridge," he offered. "I think Mrs. Jesmond left some kind of pie in there."

Willow sighed, sinking into the leather upholstery and settling. "Why don't all men proposition me like that? For God's sake, man…drive!"

● ● ● ● ●

"What's so funny?" Hugh asked, glancing at his wife as he opened his briefcase.

Madeleine looked up from the laptop. "Willow… Edward McGinnity's love interest. She's hilarious."

"So what are they up to?" He extracted the files he would review that night.

"At the moment they're driving her home after the murder."

"In a police car?"

"No…a Jag Mark II."

"Better write in a breakdown, then. It'll be more realistic."

Madeleine rolled her eyes. "Andrew happened to buy a lemon, Hugh. And he was always tinkering with the poor machine without the foggiest what he was doing." She looked around for somewhere to rest her coffee, eventually choosing the windowsill. "It's unfair to judge all Jaguars by the failings of your old flatmate's heap!"

"Whatever you say. But if there's no break down, anyone who knows anything about Jags will be immediately reminded that you're writing *fiction*!"

"The car can break down later." She returned to the computer screen. "The story's just begun."

Willow was no stranger to Edward's modern two-storey villa. Madeleine could see that from the way she walked in. The artist's eyes did not move around the room even subtly. She knew what was in it, on its walls, she knew without asking where the glasses were kept.

But then she'd helped Edward find the house in the first place, when he'd decided to move from the grand family home which had become his too young. They'd spent weeks visiting open houses, being shown through the best of the inner city real estate market, until they'd come across 19 Bayside Close, distinctly dated but located in the city's most desirable suburb.

A silver-haired agent in a navy blazer and rather too much cologne had talked to Edward about the Mark II and shown Willow directly to the kitchen, which he described as "any woman's dream." She'd declared the benches too high. "How on Earth am I going to get up here?" Willow had said, trying to hoist herself onto the island bench. "And marble's so cold on your back!"

Edward always claimed he'd bought the place out of embarrassment.

He'd gutted it then and remade it as his own.

There was Black Forest cake in the refrigerator. Edward made coffee and served the cake onto plates with generous scoops of vanilla-bean ice cream.

Willow disappeared up the iron staircase to swap Edward's jacket for something more comfortable. She descended wearing one of his sweatshirts over her cocktail dress and took both plates to the couch, placing his on the glossy surface of the coffee table beside a small Matchbox Mercedes Benz.

"You're writing something new?" she accused, picking up the toy car.

He brought in coffee in two mugs, placed them down and took the car from her. "Yes."

She gazed up at him. "So tell me?"

Edward sat beside her on the couch and told her about Madeleine d'Leon, his crime-writer.

Willow listened, eating cake as she concentrated on the picture he was building. "And so the story is about...?"

"It's an exploration of an author's relationship with her protagonist, an examination of the tenuous line between belief and reality, imagination and self, and what happens when that line is crossed."

Willow nodded gravely. "I'm not sure what that means, but it does sound award-winning."

Edward laughed.

Willow's high-arched brow furrowed slightly. "Isn't your heroine a little ordinary, Ned? Maybe you should jazz her up a bit…give her a dark past as say a stripper, or a drug dealer."

"She's a lawyer."

"I suppose that's pretty close…but, I don't know— what about a bizarre hobby? She could be a taxidermist. Taxidermists are interesting."

"She's a writer, Will."

"But how are you going to make that sustain an entire book? Opening a laptop and typing isn't exactly an action scene."

"The story's about what goes on in her head and how powerful that becomes." He took a gulp of coffee as he tried to explain. "She has to be outwardly normal. But Will, her mind is extraordinary…it's exciting."

Willow wrinkled her nose. "And here, I thought you were a legs man."

"You underestimate me." He glanced at the perfect curve of her long calves. She'd kicked off her shoes and curled them up on the couch.

She wrinkled her nose. "Never! I have no doubt this will be a literary masterpiece." Willow forked another mouthful of cake, closing her eyes and murmuring her contentment. "Tell me, what's she doing now?"

Edward put down his coffee mug. "She's waiting... in a small-town tea shop. It's one of those long rooms, with a big window at the front looking onto the street, and kitchen in the back. There're a few people there. She's ordered a skim cappuccino while she pretends to be absorbed in her notebook. You see, she still gets nervous in public spaces on her own."

"She's shy?"

"Not really...just a little self-conscious, I think. It's why she ordered the coffee...she didn't really want one yet, but she feels uncomfortable taking a table without making her intention to spend money clear in some way."

"Who's she waiting for?"

"Her literary agent."

Willow dragged a cushion behind her head and lay back, settling expectantly.

Madeleine skimmed the chocolate-encrusted foam from the top of her cappuccino, licking the sweet froth from her spoon before stirring. She checked her watch, wondering how long Leith would be.

The offices of Welcome to the Fold, Leith Henry's literary agency, were in the city, but she'd come through Ashwood for one thing or another every couple of weeks...more often, if she actually had a reason to come.

"Leith Henry? Isn't that your agent's name?" Willow asked.

"Yes."

"Isn't that a bit weird, Ned?"

"I don't see why."

"Because she's real."

"Do you want to know what Madeleine is up to or not?"

Willow rolled her eyes. "Of course I do…tell me a story, Homer."

Madeleine felt agitated, restless. She was looking forward to seeing her agent, but part of her wanted to be at home in her pyjamas, writing. It was always the way when a new idea had her in its grip—it ruined her for anything else. Madeleine knew that apart from writing, she would do nothing wholeheartedly again until the book was finished.

The tea shop door opened and a long, slender woman with a sheath of rose gold hair stepped in, waving as she did so. Madeleine moved her notebook off the table to make room as the agent peeled off her scarf, her coat and then her leather gloves, emerging from her stylish outer cocoon in a chic paisley blouse and low-slung jeans.

Madeleine wondered, fleetingly, how much time she could save if only she wore clothes as well as Leith Henry, if she could throw on anything in her cupboard, confident that it wouldn't make her look fat, or washed out, or just plain odd. As it was, Madeleine lost at least half an hour a day choosing what to wear, except those days she spent in her pyjamas writing. She smiled. Perhaps that was the source of her creative passion… a longing to wear nothing but pyjamas.

"What's funny?" Leith asked, looking over her shoulder as if she expected the answer to be there.

"Nothing," Madeleine replied. "I was just thinking of something stupid."

They chose from the menu to ensure their order was taken before the frantic lunchtime influx. Leith considered several dishes before settling on a lamb burger. Madeleine selected the chickpea salad as she always did. On matters of food, she was a creature of habit.

"I'm so sorry I'm late," Leith sighed. "I had a client ring at the last moment...the smelly one."

Dr. Leith Henry was a psychologist by trade, and still practised two days a week. She maintained that counselling was not all that different to being a literary agent—both professions were about having difficult conversations with people who could well be crazy. The smelly client apparently suffered from a form of hydrophobia which meant he was afraid to wash. He had been referred for counselling when his co-workers refused to work in the same office.

They talked for a while about the efficacy of scented candles as opposed to spray fresheners. It seemed neither had been powerful enough to mask the presence of the pungent hydrophobic.

"So," Leith began when their meals arrived, "I've read the chapter you sent me last night."

"What did you think?" Madeleine felt suddenly panicked. She wasn't sure she was ready to be professional about Edward.

"I liked it...a lot...but what happened to Veronica Killwilly?"

"Nothing's happened to Ronnie. This just isn't about her." Madeleine's shoulders tensed. She felt strangely disloyal. Veronica Killwilly was the protagonist of her previous books, a series about a housemaid who solved murders in her spare time. It was with Veronica that she had built a readership upon foundations of obscurity.

"The publishers like Veronica." Leith poured tomato sauce on her burger with the unrestrained pleasure of a child.

"Don't you think they'll like Edward?"

"They've spent a fortune building your brand."

"I'm a person, not a brand."

"Not anymore. You're Madeleine d'Leon, synonymous with the working-class, feminist heroine who solves crime by looking at what people throw away…and now you want to write about a man with more money than he knows what to do with."

"I can't just write Veronica Killwilly investigates for the rest of my life, Leith."

The agent nodded. "I know. I just want you to know how they're going to react. Especially now that there's talk of a television series."

"There's what?"

"It's early days yet. I wouldn't have mentioned it except that I want you to understand why their reaction might be less than enthusiastic."

"I don't care about their reaction. I want to know what you think."

Leith put down her knife and fork and took a sip of sparkling water.

Madeleine braced herself.

"It's different in style to your previous work," the agent said thoughtfully. "The prose is amazing, like reading poetry. Edward is intriguing, kind of sexy in a brooding sort of way. He jumps from the page. You know, Maddie, if you continue the way you've begun, I suspect it might end up your best work to date."

Madeleine warmed, breathing again. "I think so too. I can't explain it…I can see him so clearly. It's like he exists, like I'm being allowed to watch."

"Watch what?"

"His life…his mind…"

Leith laughed, shaking her head.

"You think I'm mad?"

"Yes and no…you're a writer."

"So you think I should keep going?"

"Could I stop you if I wanted to?"

"You know what I mean."

The agent extracted a notebook from her bag and opened it to make a note. "When's your next Veronica Killwilly novel due?"

"I've only just submitted the latest manuscript, so not for about a year."

"How long will you need to write it?"

"Four, maybe five months."

"Then you have about seven months to play with Mr. McGinnity. Let's see how it comes out. In the meantime, I'll speak to some publishers, see what they think about Madeleine d'Leon writing something more…well, something new."

Madeleine beamed. Edward paused. She really did have a beautiful smile. It transformed her.

Willow looked at him thoughtfully. "Why is she so caught up with this story?"

"She's a writer, it's what she does."

"But why is this story different? She's obviously written books before. Why does she become so involved with this one? I know you, Ned McGinnity. You're not going to write a simple happy tale about a crime-writer."

Edward considered for a moment. "She's lonely."

"She's married."

"Even so. I think there's a silence between her and her husband that she doesn't know how to overcome." He returned to the tea room to explain.

"Should I talk to the publishers about giving you some time off to...?" Leith began looking closely at Madeleine.

Something flickered in Madeleine's eyes. A kind of panicked sadness, a telltale glassiness.

"Hugh wants to stop trying for a while," she said. "The last miscarriage...he just thinks we should stop."

"And you? What do you think?"

"I think he's wrong...but if he doesn't want to, how can I force him, Leith?"

"Does he know how you feel?"

Madeleine shrugged.

"Have you talked about it, at least?"

"I don't know how to...it's so sad and serious. It's not us...perhaps he's right."

"You should talk to him, Maddie."

"Things are just beginning to feel normal." Madeleine tried to force her voice to sound ordinary, light. She tried to conceal the thick disappointment, the terror that this was it. "I don't want to push it. Hugh's work is really demanding at the moment." She smiled again. This time it was pensive and strained. "I'll give it a few months. Maybe once I finish this book."

"Oh, Maddie..."

"I'm just so sad for it, Leith...it would have had such a wonderful life if it had stayed...we could have given it so much...if it had stayed."

"You're not giving up, are you?" Leith asked.

"No, I'm not." Madeleine bit her lip. "Though sometimes I wonder if Hugh and I will ever...What's it like, really?"

The agent sighed happily. She had three children. "I could tell you about the awful parts, but you won't believe me. No woman ever does—it must some kind of evolutionary deafness designed to ensure the human race continues."

Madeleine waited. She'd asked Leith this question before and she needed to hear the answer again.

"It's hard to describe exactly," Leith continued. "You think you couldn't love anyone more than you love Hugh, but when you have a baby, that love will seem small and pale. You'll love Hugh more because he loves your baby, but he'll be a distant second—and you will be for him—but neither of you will mind. It's a strange, mighty all-consuming love." She sighed. "I'm glad you're not giving up." Leith frowned then, as a thought occurred. "Do you want me to talk to Hugh?"

Madeleine laughed and looked warmly at her friend. "Leith, you're my literary agent."

"I'm quite happy to insert kicking your husband's backside into my job description at no extra charge."

"Thank you, but Hugh and I will work it out... eventually."

The agent studied her, considered her. "Then we should have cake."

"Does she really think that?" Willow asked. "Your agent? About children?"

Edward nodded. "Yes. She complains that they've destroyed her life...but she does believe that."

Willow leaned forward and stole a forkful of his cake. "What do you think, Ned?"

"About kids? I don't know. I don't have any. Maybe I'll feel that way, but I can't imagine loving anyone more than—" He stopped. "I don't know."

"Elliot doesn't think it's right to bring children into a world when there are already too many people on the planet," Willow murmured, half to herself.

Madeleine could hear what Edward thought of Elliot, but of course Willow could not.

"You should do what you want to, Will," he said quietly.

She looked at him uncertainly for a moment, and then she smiled brightly, shaking off the wistfulness he'd seen just moments before. "That's not the way the world works, Ned, my darling. Elliot's probably right."

Moving On

Madeleine wasn't really sure what came next. She didn't write police procedurals for good reason. They required an insight into police practice that she didn't have. Who knew what paperwork or procedure was involved in the investigation of a murder? Who knew what happened first or how long it took? The Veronica Killwilly novels were set in 1916, the protagonist a domestic servant who investigated crime in a town the war had denuded of men. Veronica didn't work with the police and if their paths did happen to cross, the internal workings of the constabulary were glossed over with the sepia lens of history.

This was different. Edward's story was contemporary. A careless inaccuracy might pull the reader sharply from the world she was trying to create. A discordant detail could break the spell.

But what would happen next? Madeleine presumed the coroner would conduct a post-mortem, but how long would that take?

She discussed the problem with Hugh over breakfast.

"High-profile death like that would probably be rushed through," he said. "But does it really matter what the coroner says? It's not as if it could be anything but murder."

"He could have simply fallen," Madeleine replied, pouring maple syrup onto her bowl of porridge.

"Why would he have been in the fire escape? I don't think the police would need to wait for the coroner to decide it was murder."

Madeleine nodded. "You're right." She was relieved. It was not that Hugh knew any more than she about the ins and outs of police procedure, but his logic was comforting. Perhaps she could just take for granted that the police would investigate. It was what Edward McGinnity would do that interested her. Hopefully that was what readers would focus upon too.

"How did your meeting with Leith go?" Hugh asked through a mouthful of cornflakes.

Madeleine told him about the possibility of a television series. "It'll probably come to nothing."

"Your enthusiasm's a bit underwhelming, Maddie."

"I write books—television is for someone else to get worked up about."

"Still, it'd be nice to be rich. Maybe you should be concentrating on the Killwilly novels."

"Oh, Hugh, they talk about a television series every couple of years. It won't come to anything."

"But if it does, you could keep me in the style to which I'd like to become accustomed."

Maddie laughed. "Let's just wait and see, shall we?"

"Fair enough. What have you planned for today?" Hugh made a sandwich with toast and jam to take with him. He had rounds at the hospital this morning.

"I'm writing," she replied. "I might bake a cake if I get time."

"Would you like me to speak to Jeeves?"

"No. A Swiss roll from the supermarket isn't going to cut it. I feel like proper cake. Would you grab some black cherries on your way home?"

"Black cherries?"

"Just the tinned variety. I have a hankering for Black Forest cake, for some reason."

Hugh pulled a pen from his breast pocket and wrote "black cherries" on his hand. "Jeeves will be hurt, but I'll try."

Once Hugh had departed, Madeleine settled in her writing chair, an old wingback that had been worn in the just the right spots. The throw which covered it hid the tears in the plaid upholstery and a past calamity with coffee. It was positioned near the fire and a power strip, into which she plugged her laptop.

Madeleine closed her eyes and waited for Edward McGinnity, called him from that part of her soul where stories are held awaiting release.

He was just waking, rising drowsy and bare-chested from a bed that bore the dishevelled imprint of a restless night. Sitting on the edge of the bed, he pressed the heels of his palms to his eyes and rubbed his face.

Madeleine softened. In sleep the features of men became soft and innocent, and they seemed to wake as the little boys they once were.

Edward looked up and for a breath it seemed that their eyes met, locked, that they recognised one another. He smiled faintly and reached for one of the notebooks he kept on the trunk beside the bed. Rolling onto his stomach, he pulled a pillow under his chest and wrote.

Madeleine noticed the scar on his lower back then; wide and slightly raised, it ran from his spine around his torso beneath his ribcage. The accident that had killed his family—he must have been in the car, too.

Although she wondered what he remembered, Madeleine did not stop to define this part of Edward McGinnity's backstory. He would tell her when he was ready to do so…give her access to his memories some night as she was falling asleep or early in the morning when the dreams of the people in her head became her own.

The telephone rang. Edward groaned and shut the notebook. He rolled over, realising he'd left his phone on the coffee table by the couch. Taking the stairs three at a time he made it to the phone before it rang out.

"McGinnity," he said as he snatched up the receiver. "Leith…Blast! I'm so sorry. I slept in."

Madeleine typed more quickly, pleased that she'd managed to work another of her friends into Edward's story.

"Half an hour?" Edward said. "Sure…What about here? I have coffee and I think there's some cake left."

Putting down the phone, he ran back up the stairs to shower and dress, returning in jeans and a crewneck jumper under which he wore a collared shirt. He set about brewing a pot of coffee.

A knock.

"Door's open."

"Mr. McGinnity?"

Edward stepped out of the kitchen. "Who are you?"

The man standing just inside his threshold wore a too-fitted suit with an open-collared shirt. He smelled of deodorant applied excessively. A second man, in a Dr. Who t-shirt, stood at the open door with a video camera and boom mike. "What the dickens—?" Edward began.

"I was hoping you could answer a few questions, Mr. McGinnity."

"Questions? About what?"

"About the death of Mr. Vogel, sir."

"Who are you?"

"Peter Blake, sir. I'm from Channel Six."

"You're a reporter?"

"Would you mind answering a few questions about last night, Mr. McGinnity?"

"Yes, I would mind."

"Is it true that Miss Meriwether threatened the deceased?"

"Of course not. I think you should leave."

"Is it true that the police consider Miss Meriwether a person of interest?"

"Get out!"

"Were you aware that Mr. Vogel had submitted a very negative review of Miss Meriwether's exhibition?"

The question distracted Edward from his intention to throw the man out. "How could he have? He died at the opening."

"It seems a number of critics were given an advance viewing so that their reviews could come out as soon as possible. Mr. Vogel was delivering Channel Six's Arts Report, so you can understand we're taking a particular interest."

Edward regarded the reporter coldly. "You're trespassing. Leave."

"You invited me in, Mr. McGinnity."

"Get out before I throw you out!"

"Are you threatening me, Mr. McGinnity?"

"Yes, I am."

"Ned!" Leith Henry sidestepped the cameraman and walked into the house. "What's going on here?"

Edward threw his arms in the air. "Reporters. They won't leave."

Leith looked sternly at the men from Channel Six. "Gentlemen, Mr. McGinnity has asked you to leave and now he has a witness you can't edit out."

Blake opened his mouth to reply, then seemed to think better of it. He pulled out a card and placed it on the hall table. "We really are interested in finding out what actually happened, Mr. McGinnity. Geoffrey Vogel was a much-loved personality and a personal friend."

"I'm afraid that particular friendship does nothing to recommend you, sir," Edward snarled.

Blake bristled, but he replied evenly. "Please call me when you're ready to tell your side of the story."

Leith cleared her throat and looked towards the door. Blake conceded, backing out.

"What the hell did he mean by my side?" Edward asked as Leith shut and bolted the door.

"Why did you let them in?"

"I thought it was you. God, sorry…you don't even know…"

"Yes, I do." Leith pulled a newspaper from her bag. The death of Geoffrey Vogel was splashed across the front page. "It looks like you had quite the evening."

Edward took the paper and scanned the article. Clearly someone had spoken to the media.

He sighed. "Coffee?"

Leith nodded. "Well said."

Leith salvaged the remains of cake from the refrigerator whilst Edward poured coffee. As he did so he read the article in the *Herald*, which reported the murder and eulogised the television arts presenter and renowned literary editor. The piece credited Geoffrey Vogel with having a hand in the careers of some of the nation's greatest writers and artists. It alleged a bitter falling-out between Willow Meriwether and Vogel, precipitated by his critique of her exhibition as "shallow and lacking originality."

"Bloody hypocrite," Edward muttered.

Leith pulled a stool up to the kitchen bench, placed the cake between them and handed him a fork. "You'd better tell me what happened last night."

Edward did so.

"So Vogel and Meriwether weren't at odds, as far as you could see?"

"No. He couldn't tell her enough how wonderful she was…thought one of her paintings was a tribute to him."

"And was it?"

"God, no! It was a painting of my desk. Will stayed here for a week when she was fighting with Elliot last year. She painted the couch, the coat stand, and my bed as well, I think."

"Your bed?" Leith grinned.

"I wasn't in it…and neither was she." Edward laughed. "Will has an obsession with furniture—it's an art thing."

Leith read through the article again. "You aren't mentioned, so let's just wait and see. If your friend from Channel Six decides to bring you into it somehow, we may have to issue a press release."

"What about Will?"

"Adrian Barrington is her agent isn't he?"

"Yes."

"He knows what he's doing, Ned. He's probably already dealt with it." She rummaged through her handbag and extracted a notebook and pen. "Forget about all that. We need to talk about you." Leith looked at him, glowing.

"What?" he said recognising a certain triumph in her manner.

"I've found a publisher for *Sentience*."

Edward stared at her in horror. *Sentience* had been his first novel. It had been signed by a major publishing house before Geoffrey Vogel had destroyed it. Edward had come to hate what his novel had become…he'd pulled it from publication himself. Buried it. Leith had somehow kept him from being sued by the publishing house. "Leith, what have you done?"

Leith placed a hand on his arm. "I sent the original manuscript, Ned. I kept an unedited version—as you wrote it. They liked it, they want it, and you will have full editorial control. They won't change a comma without your say-so."

"Who?"

"Barn Owl Books. They're not a mega publisher but they have a good reputation. They can't offer you the same advance you had with Middleton Meyer but they love the story as it is, Ned. They want to get it ready for an August release."

Edward said nothing for a moment. He had nearly given away writing after the train wreck of his experience with *Sentience*. He had been published since, to significant acclaim, but he'd mourned *Sentience*. He had walked away from it of his own volition, but there was something haunting about a story abandoned, characters and ideas denied the light of day. His novels since had not been written with quite the same naivety and consequent joy...until Madeleine.

Madeleine held her breath. She wanted him to be happy about this, but she wasn't sure...he wasn't sure.

Edward exhaled. "Okay, thank you."

"This is good news," Leith said.

"I know. But it's rather like being told that someone is coming back from the dead years after you finally let them go...it takes a little getting used to."

Madeleine saw then. He'd written his own tragedy into *Sentience*, his family, his grief. No wonder he was so winded by its resurrection.

"You want to see it published, don't you Ned?" Leith asked.

"Yes, I guess so. I haven't looked at it in a couple of years...but yes."

"Good. I'll organise the contracts. In the meantime, suppose you tell me what you're working on."

"How did you know I was—?"

"I can see it in your eyes...a distraction. You're not all here."

"Not all here? Charming."

"Don't pretend to be offended. Who are you with?"

Edward told her about Madeleine. Leith listened.

"You don't think this novel will be too self-referential?"

He shrugged. "All novels are self-referential to some extent."

Leith stood and opened his refrigerator. Her smile was knowing, teasing. "Look at you...you're excited."

"Shut up." Edward was suddenly embarrassed.

She laughed at him. "Have you started? Do you have something I can look at?"

"Yes, I've started, but I'm not ready for you to look. I don't want to break the spell, Leith. This might be the best thing I've ever written."

Leith rolled her eyes. "Writers! I ask for a manuscript and you start mumbling about black magic." She took an unopened bottle of champagne from the refrigerator and placed it on the bench. "Very well...keep it to yourself for now, but I want you to show me something soon."

Edward saluted.

"I'm serious," she said. "Now find some glasses so we can toast *Sentience*."

• • ● • •

Madeleine barely noticed when Hugh returned. She had been languishing in the world of Edward McGinnity all day. A collection of used coffee mugs marked the hours she had spent at the laptop.

"You let the fire go out." Hugh opened the door of the cast-iron fireplace. "It's freezing in here."

"Oh, sorry. I didn't notice. It must have only just died down."

Hugh put his hand on the firebox. "It's stone cold, Maddie."

"Really? Sorry."

Hugh struck a match to light kindling and revive the flames. "I suppose I should see about tea."

Madeleine wrinkled her nose. It was a veiled reproach. Hugh had expected she'd organise something. He'd been at work all day while she was at home.

"I'll take care of it," she said closing the laptop. "You watch the news while I rustle something up." She tossed him the remote control as she headed to the kitchen with no idea what she'd cook. Her culinary skills were rudimentary at the best of times. She opened the freezer compartment and stared in. Frozen pies—they'd do. Madeleine popped three into the oven and, having found salvation in the freezer once, returned there in search of accompaniments. A bag of frozen vegetables rewarded her faith, and its contents were duly dropped into a double boiler.

Edward wrote the manner in which she tidied aimlessly while the pies warmed, the fact that she remained in the kitchen rather than returning to the living room. There was a faint, almost imperceptible trepidation in the choice. Edward studied her, poked at her barely noticeable unease. He didn't think she was afraid of Hugh…so what else? What was it she'd told Leith?…"things have just got back to normal"… Was she afraid that so little could derail normality? Edward tapped the end of his pencil against his chin, contemplating the nature of this vulnerability. Perhaps this was what would draw her to him.

And so he stayed with her while she prepared the meal, until Madeleine was able to return to Hugh with a peace offering of dinner.

Having been soothed by half an hour of national news, Hugh Lamond seemed less prickly. And he liked pies. Over dinner he told Madeleine about the rigours of his day, the politics of the hospital, and the frustrations of patient care. At some point he stood and paced.

Madeleine didn't say a great deal. When in this murky mood, Hugh required an ear, not counsel. The problems were not necessarily solvable anyway. The system would probably always be unwieldy and people would probably always be difficult. Joe Oswald's condition had not yet improved, and neither had his wife's situation. Hugh rubbed his face wearily. Mrs. Oswald had taken up half his morning in laments and hysteria, but how could he turn her away? He'd used the ten minutes he'd had for lunch to find a solicitor to draw up power of attorney documents to ensure that they would never be in such a desperate place.

Again there was reproach in the words. Madeleine wished now she'd drafted the documents herself. It would have been one less thing that Hugh had to do. Perhaps she really wasn't pulling her weight.

After they'd cleared the dinner plates, Madeleine opened the can of black cherries Hugh had brought home and they ate it with chocolate ice cream. It was close enough to Black Forest cake and required a lot less in terms of effort.

Madeleine reopened her laptop.

"Did you get much writing done today?" Hugh asked. His tone was friendly, conciliatory. Perhaps he'd sensed her hesitation.

Madeleine nodded. "Yes, it's been a good day."

"Has he solved the crime yet, your writer?"

Madeleine regarded him disdainfully. "It'd be a pretty dull book if he'd worked it out already."

"I suppose the hero of a detective novel must necessarily be a little stupid."

Madeleine knew he was baiting her. "Yes...perhaps I should make him a doctor, after all."

Trouble Begins

Edward was cooking breakfast when he received the call. He'd run that morning, more out of a need to meter his mind than any particular yen for exercise. The pounding rhythm of his own stride slowed his thoughts, shook them, so that they settled into some form of order.

He'd returned sweaty and ravenous, showering quickly and raiding the kitchen in nothing but a towel. Mrs. Jesmond didn't come on weekends, rendering both the act and the attire in which he chose to do it, if not necessary, at least acceptable.

Edward extracted eggs, bacon, pineapple, and spinach from the refrigerator and a loaf of sourdough from the cupboard and fried it all. The result was quite surprisingly edible, or so he thought, sampling directly from the pan.

The phone call, however, meant that his culinary efforts were for naught. Edward turned off the hot plate as he spoke, and ran upstairs to dress the moment he'd placed down the receiver.

Jeans and t-shirt donned in seconds, finding his car keys took a couple of minutes, and then he left the house for the home of Willow Meriwether. He didn't make it in time.

Elliot Kaufman answered the door of the run-down terrace. He wore paint-splattered overalls—the bib and brace kind—his broad, sculpted chest bare beneath. A red bandanna covered his hair. Madeleine detailed the artist quickly: the disdainful arch of his brow, the slight curl of pity—perhaps contempt—in his lips. Elliot knew Edward McGinnity loved his wife. It pleased him, having something another man coveted. "What the fuck are you doing here, McGinnity?"

Edward didn't flinch. Kaufman had always spoken like a fourteen-year-old who'd just discovered profanity. "Will called me. She said the police—"

"They've taken her in for questioning." Kaufman left the door open and walked back into the house.

For a moment Edward hesitated and then he followed the man in. The house was what Willow and Kaufman called their "space." Every room doubled as a studio, furniture lost amongst easels and stacks of canvases. A kind of creative melee in the midst of which two artists lived. "Why have they taken her in?" Edward asked.

Kaufman shrugged. "Fucked if I know—some new evidence about last night. Shall I get her to call you when she gets back?"

"I might go to the police station. Do you want a lift?"

"Where?"

"To the station."

"Fuck, no. Will's a big girl."

"Don't you think you should—?"

"I think *you* should mind your own fucking business, McGinnity."

The exchange escalated from there. Madeleine observed more than wrote. She was not really interested in Elliot Kaufman. His character was simple, motivated by arrogance and envy. It was Edward's reaction she cared about, his anger, his fury that he had lost Willow to a man who treated her like she was nothing.

"Willow is my fucking wife," Kaufman sneered. "At the moment, she may be flattered, amused by your simpering devotion, but I can guarantee you, mate, that in time she will find it as fucking pathetic as I do. We'll laugh about it in our old age after she's spread her legs for me—"

Edward hit him then. "She's your wife. Well done. You've won. Now why don't you act like you remotely deserve to have her!"

"Jesus fucking Christ!" Elliot wiped the blood from his nose. "I'll be speaking to the fucking police, all right, McGinnity. But it won't have anything to do with bloody Willow. Now get the fuck out!"

Madeleine felt strangely startled as Edward walked away, Kaufman swearing and threatening in his wake. This was a turn she'd not expected. The level of vitriol between the two was not something she'd planned; it was too extreme to ignore. Elliot Kaufman was going to force his way into this story, however minor she had intended to write his part. She left the artist and followed the writer.

Edward McGinnity drove directly to the police station. He took a deep breath before stepping out of the Jaguar, reining in his fury. Willow had no idea how much he and Kaufman loathed each other. They had competed for her hand and he had lost. Now his friendship with Willow depended on her believing he'd accepted that. Kaufman knew better, of course, but he, too, maintained the farce because it suited his need to gloat.

The constable with whom Edward spoke was young, condescendingly cheerful. She directed him to take a seat in the public waiting room.

Edward sat down beside a woman who had probably never been a girl. Her mouth curved fleetingly, scarlet lipstick on thin lips, broad shoulders hunched self-consciously. He said "Good morning," and they both fell into a polite disengagement. The waiting room of a police station was probably not the best place to make friends.

"Edward? Edward McGinnity?"

Edward's head snapped up towards the voice.

A middle-aged woman at the front desk, her bob proudly silver, her figure solid, her stance wide and steady. She left the forms she'd been filling out. Edward stood, unconsciously stepping back.

Her eyes softened, and she smiled as she approached him. "It is you, isn't it?"

He nodded. Edward hadn't seen Charlotte Adelaide in years but he hadn't forgotten her. They'd first met fifteen years ago in the hospital. She'd been at his bedside when he came out of the anaesthesia. She'd told him that his entire family was dead. He'd been thirteen, and she'd been assigned as his social worker.

Madeleine closed the laptop. She needed to stop. To take a moment in the face of such overwhelming grief. To work out how she would put it into words...if it could be put into words. It was time to make coffee.

But the look on Edward McGinnity's face did not leave her. Not as she made coffee, nor as she drank. Not as she scrolled through her e-mails, answering the urgent and the interesting. Even after all these years, the broken horror in Edward's eyes clutched at her chest. She fortified herself with another cup of coffee and a hunk of chocolate before returning to her laptop.

Charlotte Adelaide caught Edward in a maternal embrace, which was startling in its strength. Resisting would have been futile.

"Well, look at you, sweetie, all grown up. I always knew you'd be a handsome man. I had hoped never to encounter you in a place like this, but considering what you've been through…"

"I'm waiting for a friend, Miss Adelaide."

"Drugs?" she whispered. "Is it drugs? I know of some excellent programs…"

"I'm waiting for a friend," Edward said again. "She's giving a statement."

The social worker studied him, and deciding suddenly that he was telling the truth, she tittered. "Oh, dear. I thought…forgive me, Edward. It's a professional habit. How have you been? What are you doing with yourself now?"

"I…I write."

"Books? How wonderful! I've always thought I should write a book—the things I've seen! If it weren't for the legalities…"

Edward smiled. "I have no doubt."

"Your friend…who you're waiting for…is it drugs?"

"No, I'm afraid not."

Charlotte Adelaide sighed, disappointed. "Pity. I could have helped, if so." She rummaged in her bulging handbag and eventually extracted a packet of Mentos. She grabbed his hand and dropped a couple of sweets into it, before popping another into her own mouth.

Edward stared at the white pellets, turning them over in his hand as the social worker prattled on. God, it was familiar. The background noise of Charlotte Adelaide and her Mentos. And that feeling...like he was hollow. He shook his head to dislodge the memory, to bring himself back from the edge of that yawning hole into which everything he had known and loved and trusted had fallen.

But the social worker would not allow it, reminiscing relentlessly, catching him up on the foster families with whom he had been placed initially. They were grey in his memory, and vague. Like an idea never seriously considered. But he had been so consumed with grief and guilt and anger then that the world had receded out of his reach, out of his comprehension. Perhaps the foster families had been kind, perhaps they had tried to love him...he couldn't remember.

Madeleine gazed at the words on her screen, trying to pull away. This was backstory. A novice writer's mistake. And yet she could not leave it alone. She had to know what had happened to the orphaned boy. How had he lived? Who had sent him to school? Who had cared about him...comforted him?

"Tell me love, how is Mr. Finlay?" Charlotte Adelaide enquired, sitting down in the waiting room and patting the plastic chair beside her.

Slowly Edward took the seat, the Mentos still in his hand. "He's in London—some kind of sabbatical, I believe."

"Oh, is he? I expect you're still close. I can tell you it was a weight off my mind when he agreed to take you in. You were happy there, weren't you, Edward?" The question was tentative.

"Yes," Edward replied. It wasn't entirely true. He hadn't been happy for a long time after the accident, but he had been less unhappy with Andrew Finlay.

An associate of his father's, Finlay had appointed himself Edward's lawyer. He'd sued a number of multinationals on his young client's behalf, faceless conglomerates who had built the bridge which had collapsed under a passing car and wiped out all but one member of a family.

The barrister was not family, but he had been familiar at a time when Edward needed something from before. It was only after a succession of unsuccessful foster placements, that the courts had allowed Edward McGinnity to live with his lawyer. Finlay did not attempt to father him. They'd been housemates of a kind, friends in a master and apprentice sort of way.

The various lawsuits were eventually settled the year Edward attained majority, for a sum that ensured both he and Finlay would thereafter be rich men. Still, Edward had never considered his fortune to be good fortune; it was just one of the things that happened after everyone died.

He checked his watch, unsure what to say. He knew almost nothing about Charlotte Adelaide. Was there a husband or children about whom to politely enquire? A dog? A cat? Edward had no idea. She had brought him the news that his family was dead, and held his hand until he had been able to breathe. He had no doubt that she'd genuinely cared, but when he'd finally moved beyond his grief, he'd left her behind. Charlotte Adelaide had somehow become fused with his loss. Seeing her now made him feel bad in so many ways.

She gave him her card, the cheaply printed generic business cards issued by the Department. He promised himself that he would send her flowers and a note.

She reached over and patted his hand. "I'd better get back to my client," she said. "It's been lovely seeing you, pet. I'm so glad you found your way. I'll pop into the library tomorrow and ask for your books—you'll be the first famous author I actually know."

He stood. "It was nice to see you too, Ms. Adelaide."

Perhaps she knew he was lying. The social worker smiled sadly and returned to the counter and her forms, while Edward resumed the plastic seat to wait for Willow. He felt sick, congested with the memory of first knowing. It was like bile, bitter. He gagged, closing his eyes and breathing. This was ridiculous…it had been fifteen years. And yet suddenly, he once again felt completely, overwhelmingly alone.

And then a gaze locked on his, though he'd not yet opened his eyes. Her gaze—Madeleine's, her presence. He wasn't sure why he was thinking of her now, but he was glad. If he focussed on her—this literary construct of his—perhaps the panic would subside. She would give him something else to think about, a reason to step away from the abyss of remembering.

Edward exhaled slowly, and pulled back, just enough so he could see more than the warm brown of her eyes. Madeleine d'Leon wore pyjamas. She was writing. He pulled back further. There was something else he wanted to see. She'd mentioned a miscarriage…he knew already that it had changed her. He needed to know. And so he looked for her two years before.

Madeleine wore jeans now, an oversized cotton jumper with a scorch hole in the back where she'd stood too close to the fire, and well-weathered work boots as she pushed an ancient lawnmower over the paddock grass that masqueraded as a garden lawn. The day was crisp, the kind of sunbathed day that follows a frost. The light seemed cleaner somehow, the air sharp. The perfume of jonquils overlaid the duller earthy scent of newly cut, slightly wet grass.

Madeleine pressed a hand to her cheek. She could feel the heat in her face. She cut the mower's engine, moving slowly, heavily and sat on the rough steps which led from a small verandah. It was only then that she noticed the splotchy rash on her arms—a reaction to the roses she'd been pruning, no doubt.

Standing, she rubbed the stiffness from her neck. Every small movement seemed to take effort at the moment, but perhaps that was the pregnancy. Her body was preoccupied with creating another person from scratch. It could hardly be expected to have energy for gardening as well. She smiled, cradling the thought of the new life within her. It was like having some magic secret protected inside her body, but, of course, it wasn't a secret. Hugh knew, though he wouldn't talk about it, was determined to ignore it for as long as possible.

Madeleine longed to talk about names and look for prams, but his lack of enthusiasm made her feel silly, and so she held off.

She shrugged off her disappointment with him. Hugh would come around and then they would be excited together. It was not as if the pregnancy was an accident. They'd agreed. Madeleine shook her head. Men were strange creatures.

She walked inside and filled a mug from the tap. My God, she was tired. She looked again at the blotchy rash on her forearms. It was odd. She'd never had a reaction like that before. Perhaps a shower would wash off whatever pollen it was that was irritating her skin.

It was not till she slipped off her work jeans that she saw the blotches on her thighs and then her stomach. A small flutter of panic buried quickly. Hadn't she read that strange rashes and reactions were perfectly normal in pregnancy?

Madeleine showered and lay down on the couch with a morning talk show. Bantering hosts with gleaming hair and teeth. Determined not to become one of those women who turned to glass the moment they became pregnant, Madeleine ignored her own uneasiness. The rash seemed more marked now, but that was probably the effect of the hot water.

The end was signalled by blood a little later. Madeleine wasn't sure what to do. She knew what was happening, but she wasn't certain what should follow. Hugh was with a patient, unavailable. She left a message. And she called her own doctor. He said that it did sound like she was having a miscarriage and told her to come in the next morning.

And so Edward alone watched as Madeleine d'Leon's baby was lost, as from her heart slipped the quiet excitement that had nested there. He watched as she wept, ever so briefly, wiping her face and pulling herself together, containing her horror too quickly. This sort of thing happened all the time. It was not a big deal and a good job they had not made an announcement or bought a pram.

When Hugh finally came home, they quarrelled over what to have for dinner. She picked the fight. He was trying to be nice, to cheer her up with Chinese food— a sweet and sour salve. After all she seemed to be handling it well, philosophically without undue histrionics. Miscarriages weren't uncommon in the first trimester…it didn't need to mean anything catastrophic. And Madeleine felt alone with her sadness—this was her loss, not his. Hugh was funny and comforting and not devastated. Here first began the thought that the baby had sensed its father's lack of enthusiasm, that somehow that had influenced its decision not to stay.

But Madeleine knew that was silly, unfair. And so she was just angry.

Edward searched for the words to adequately describe the strange grief that gripped Madeleine, a sense that something had been left behind. A child who died before it could be truly loved. Perhaps that was the difference. Madeleine felt her own child's grief, its sense of the life it had been denied, Hugh only their own disappointment.

Desserts

Her doctor gave her antibiotics, some pamphlets, and a speech on grief, loss, and depression. Madeleine smiled and told him she was fine. She was only ten weeks along after all. She stopped by the garden centre on the way home and bought box hedges and a weeping cherry tree, a cement plinth and a statue to sit upon it. A sleeping cherub, a fat Botticelli baby. She shook her head, mortified by the fact that she was turning into a cliché. God, how embarrassing. But still, she wanted the statue.

They delivered her purchases that afternoon and she began to build the garden. A secret memorial so the poor small thing would know it was grieved a little at least. But no one else must know because this was silly.

"Ned."

Willow's voice pulled Edward from Madeleine's garden. She looked tired and frightened as she stood at the desk signing forms. Bourke loomed beside her, pointing to the places on the form which required her signature.

"Is this where you tell me not to leave town, Detective?" she asked—a forced facetiousness, a brittle bravado.

Edward put his arm around her. "Will, are you all right?"

Bourke left them to it. It was only then she broke down, burying her face in Edward's shoulder so the desk sergeant would not see.

Edward said nothing, manoeuvring her out of the station in the protection of his arms. Outside he gave her his handkerchief.

Madeleine lingered over the gesture, the fact that a man of his age even carried a handkerchief. There was something archaically gallant about the way he handed it to her, like the old-fashioned manner in which he cursed. She wondered where that came from. There was a sense to Edward McGinnity that seemed to run counter to the past she'd given him. She pondered what she didn't yet know.

Edward took Willow to a quiet restaurant. He ordered tea and all the desserts on the menu. The waiter asked only if they'd like the desserts served on a single tray. Edward nodded. "We'd better have some ice cream in the middle."

"Naturally, sir."

Madeleine laughed, aware she was romanticising her protagonist ludicrously. Who wouldn't fall in love with a man who'd order all the desserts on offer? That on its own made Edward McGinnity irresistible.

Willow began with the chocolate mousse, Edward the citrus-almond cake on his side of the tray. She told him about the interrogation then, the endless questions, repeated and restructured so she became confused and tongue-tied.

"They think I pushed him, Ned."

"God...why?"

"They found part of his review of my show in the stairs, a torn fragment of a draft."

"So?"

"They say he showed me the review...that I got angry, tore it up, and pushed him down the stairs." Willow cut the brandied pear in half and pushed one section towards Edward. "Detective Bourke kept promising I could say it was an accident...that I didn't intend for him to fall. I just got so flustered..."

Edward swallowed his share of the pear. "Why didn't you ask for a lawyer, Will?"

"I don't know." Her voice was hoarse. "I didn't want to seem...I don't know. Who would I have called, Ned? I don't know any lawyers."

"You would have called me and I would have done the rest. We'll find you a lawyer today. I'll ring Andy."

"Isn't he overseas?" Willow reminded Madeleine of what she'd written before.

"Yes, but he's due back in a day or two. At the very least he'll be able to give us the name of someone to call."

"Ned, we can't afford—"

"I can, so you can."

"Elliot wouldn't like—"

"I don't care."

"Ned—"

"Will, he wouldn't even come to the station."

"I told him not to."

Edward took a breath, stopped himself before he broke and told her that Elliot was beneath her, that he did not deserve her. "Will, you should have a lawyer. We'll come to some arrangement about the money.

Do this for me. I need to know that you've got the best representation possible."

"I didn't do anything, Ned."

"I know. A good lawyer will be able to make sure it's sorted out quickly, without your name ending up in the papers." He flinched a little as he said the last, thinking of the reporter from the day before. It might already be too late for that.

They argued about the lawyer through a rhubarb clafoutis and the vanilla bean pana cotta, but the crème caramel saw Willow give in as Edward knew she would. He saw from the beginning that she was scared beyond pride.

Willow considered the demolished remains of the tray of desserts. "Call Mr. Finlay," she said. "Ask if he'll speak to me as soon as I come out of my sugar-induced coma."

Edward nodded. "It'll be all right, Will."

"I don't want to talk about this anymore." She wiped her eye with the heel of her hand. "Tell me about your book. How are you and your crime-writer finding each other?"

"We're rubbing along."

"Tell me, is she terribly macabre? Does she read the obituaries for research?"

"Hmmm, hadn't thought of that. Perhaps she should."

Madeleine smiled at the thought. People always assumed obituaries contained much more detail about the manner of the deceased's passing than they actually did.

Willow shook her head. "Oh, Ned, it's a good thing you're single."

"What? Why?" Edward contemplated being offended.

"Well, look at you! You're completely smitten with a figment of your imagination. A real woman wouldn't have a chance."

Edward laughed. "She's married. Even my figment is married."

"You could write an end to that. Kill him off or something." Willow's eyes gleamed wickedly. "You could have her do him in herself."

"She's the crime-writer, not me," Edward said, though he knew she was teasing him. "Besides, she loves him. It's important that she loves him."

"But does her husband love her?"

"Yes, but I think not enough."

Madeleine stopped, staring at the screen. What made him say that, what made her think that? She highlighted the text but faltered at pressing delete. It was what he'd said. She couldn't unthink it now.

"I'm afraid that's usually the case." Willow frowned. She rubbed his sleeve. "It's lovely to see that look in your eye again, Ned. I haven't seen it that strong since *Sentience*."

It was only then that Edward remembered he hadn't told her about the change in his first novel's fortunes. He put right the oversight, and she cheered and celebrated completely, despite the trouble in her own life. And he loved her more.

Madeleine closed her eyes, languishing in the way he looked at the young artist. Did men look at women like that in real life, or was she conjuring something wishful and impossibly romantic in the heart of Edward

McGinnity? Had anyone ever looked at her like that? She pulled her mind from that thought, lest it take hold.

Madeleine closed the laptop, blanching as she checked her watch. She was going to be late.

Tearing into the bedroom she exchanged her writing pyjamas for jeans, a pinstriped blouse, and her navy jacket. Not an exciting outfit, but reliable. On good days it suited her, on bad days it didn't look awful.

She pulled her car out of the drive and turned left towards Warradale, about an hour's drive away. The road was quiet as country roads tend to be, though there were places where experience told her to be vigilant for roos or wallabies intent on meeting an untimely end by leaping across in front of the only car that may have come that way in hours.

The journey gave her another hour with Edward. Just with him. When her laptop was open, she was writing his story, sharing him with plot and theme, and…well, others. When she was driving, unable to write, she could just be with him. Wonder about him. And linger over the smaller parts of his life that would never make it to print. She liked that. This hour she found snippets of his childhood before the crash. The brother who was his best friend and frequent nemesis. Games, name-calling, half-earnest tussles. She named him. Jacob McGinnity, brother of Edward. What part he'd have in this story she wasn't sure. Perhaps none at all. Perhaps she just needed to know him, how he was with Edward, so that she could know Edward.

The house outside which Madeleine pulled up was not extraordinary. Neither modern nor quaintly old, it existed in the no-man's-land of the dated. Its colours were inoffensive, its architecture bland. But the building was surrounded by a garden that was as extravagant as the structure was unremarkable. Roses competed for space with trumpet vines, lantern flowers, and a perplexing number of arbours, garden gnomes, and trellises. Madeleine had always thought her father's house an overdressed wallflower trying to hide her plainness with a loud, blowsy skirt.

She entered through the side gate to avoid the sprinklers, waving as her grandmother came out onto the porch. The old woman wore a sari.

"Hello, Aach-chi. I'm sorry I'm late."

Edward put down his pen. Realisation. Surprise. Why had he not noticed that Madeleine had eastern heritage? She was brown. He could see it when he looked at her now, but he hadn't noticed it before. She looked a little like Harijini, the Sri Lankan exchange student he'd known at school. Gosh, he'd forgotten about Harijini till now. This might add an interesting twist if he could pull it off.

"Twist?" Madeleine laughed at him. "Maybe it's just who I am…Anglo-Saxon isn't the only normal."

Edward blanched. "You're right. Sorry."

"Harijini, come in, come in," the old woman clucked.

Madeleine exhaled. She hated her second name, but her grandmother insisted on using it because it was the Sinhalese. There were lovely Sinhalese names. Sadly her parents had chosen the ugliest one possible. She sometimes wondered if her militantly western mother had done that intentionally, to ensure her daughter would use Madeleine.

"You have got a little fat!" Madeleine's grandmother led her into the kitchen. "Any good signs yet, Pu-thaa?"

"No."

"You mustn't put it off too long, you know. I had a cousin who was waited until she was old and then she couldn't conceive. Everyone was laughing. What to do?"

"Where's Dad, Aach-chi?" Madeleine let her grandmother's prattle slip into the ether. There was no point arguing with her.

"He's walked to get the newspaper. I've told him, why don't you have them deliver? But he won't listen."

"He enjoys the walk, Aach-chi."

"No wonder he's so thin!" She poured boiling water from the kettle into a battered tin teapot. "I made some bibikkan for you. Come, eat. I haven't been able to eat anything in days. The doctors don't know what is wrong with me."

Madeleine murmured sympathetically but without undue alarm as she sat at the vinyl-clothed kitchen table. The central vase of plastic roses, complete with artificial dewdrops, had graced the table since she was about six. Their centres had collected a little dust but their colour was unfaded, chemically fixed for eternity.

Edward studied the room, reading Madeleine into its peach and lemon walls. The furniture was oddly mismatched, more discordant than eclectic. Like every piece had been chosen in isolation with no regard for what else would be in the room. Photographs were displayed in gold gilt frames—Madeleine in mortar board and colours, and then again in her wedding dress. A family portrait taken many years before. Madeleine with her front teeth missing, a handsome man, middle-aged in a suit, his smile white against his dark skin, and a woman with closely cropped black hair. So this was Madeleine's DNA.

She had not mentioned her mother as yet.

"She left—when I was small."

"Why?"

"One day, she stopped being happy. Aach-chi came to live with us then…or maybe just before. I can't really remember."

"Do you see her?"

"She died of cancer five years ago."

"Do you miss her?"

"I miss what she should have been."

Madeleine's grandmother broke in, detailing the promises she'd made to God in exchange for a great-grandchild. She was sure the Almighty would be tempted by her latest offer, but it was important that Madeleine try not to irritate Him.

The door opened and a man came in with a sheaf of newspapers folded and clamped under his arm. Elmo Dhanusinghe was perhaps sixty, well-groomed and straight-backed. His voice was refined, and slightly accented. "Madeleine," he said smiling. "How long have you been here?"

"Only a few minutes, Dad. How are you?"

He sat at the table and the old woman stood to pour him a cup of tea. He asked Madeleine about her latest manuscript, winking as his mother clicked her tongue disapprovingly.

Madeleine rolled her eyes. Her grandmother had got it into her head that writing crime was somehow affecting her fertility. She told her father a little about her new protagonist, though she was vague, strangely protective. He listened eagerly.

"I don't know how you do it, Madeleine," he declared when she finished. "Where you get these ideas! I sold three of your books yesterday, by the way."

"Really, to whom?" Madeleine tried not to laugh. Her father was unquestionably her most evangelical fan. He bought extra copies of her books to foist upon those who were silly enough to answer in the affirmative when he asked, "Do you read?" And nowadays he asked that question of everyone he met.

"A client of mine. I got her an excellent return."

Madeleine groaned. She could almost hear the chatter among her father's tax clients. "He's a great accountant but you'll have to buy his daughter's books. Still, he'll probably find a way to classify it as a work-related expense."

"Did you hear, Rumani Fernando won that big prize? I can't think what it's called…"

"The Sydney Book Prize," Madeleine said naming one of the country's premier literary awards.

"She's a Sri Lankan girl," her father pointed out. "Sri Lankan writers are considered very good, you know. I think this new book of yours will be the one to win prizes."

Madeleine sighed. "Literary prizes go to literary writers, Dad. I write crime fiction."

"Why shouldn't you win?"

"My novels aren't really the worthy kind."

"Your English is very good…excellent!"

"I'm not thin enough."

"What has that got to do—?"

"Literary writers must be stick-thin, Dad." Madeleine's eyes were grave as she delivered the blow. "The women, anyway."

"What nonsense!"

"No, it's the rules." There was just the slightest crinkle at the corners of Madeleine's eyes. "To be eligible for the Sydney Book Prize you must look as though you've been so consumed by your art that you've forgotten to eat for at least a few weeks, that you been starved into clarity." She shrugged. "I could diet but Aach-chi keeps making bibikkan."

Edward chuckled. It was an absurd observation—something he'd not noticed noticing—but literary writers did tend to look as though they may well have been starving in a garret. Now that the idea had been put into his head, he couldn't think of one fat female literary writer of note. And suddenly he was hungry. He put down his pen and made himself a sandwich.

A Necessary Violence

Perhaps it was the conversation with her father, a contrary reaction to his insistence that she would win every literary award known to man, but Madeleine was suddenly anxious to add pace to Edward McGinnity's story. To assert a crime-writer's identity over the manuscript. She read over what she'd already written and there was nothing but the odd typographical error that she was moved to change, but in terms of crime fiction, the plot had not travelled far. There was a body, her protagonist had been entangled and given a reason to investigate, but the story lacked a sense of urgency. Edward was as yet too laid back, too comfortable.

The American novelist Raymond Chandler had advocated resolving such things by having a man come through the door with a gun. In her past work, Madeleine adapted the advice by introducing a new corpse every time the story slowed, but for this manuscript she thought the original advice would work better. It needed a sense of menace. She would have to put Edward McGinnity in actual physical danger.

But from whom? And why?

"I'm just a poor boy from a poor family…" Hugh Lamond wandered into the living room singing "Bohemian Rhapsody"—badly.

"Queen…really?" Madeleine winced.

"Damn radio. I can't get that bloody song out of my head," he offered by way of excuse. "Oh, you got the fire going?" Hugh removed his jacket. "I thought we were out of wood."

"We were. I split some."

"Oh, I'll go cut some more now."

"No need, I split enough for tonight."

Hugh rolled up his sleeves and picked up the second wood basket. "I'll get some more just in case."

Madeleine smiled to herself. Hugh seemed to take the fact that she could wield a log-splitter as an assault on his masculinity. Funny creatures, men.

He returned in about twenty minutes with a burgeoning wood basket and the news that he'd stacked about three days' worth on the verandah so that she wouldn't get caught short again.

Madeleine didn't argue. There was a good measure of thoughtfulness mixed in with the quaint masculine pride behind his actions, and she wasn't particularly fond of splitting wood.

"What's wrong?" he asked looking at her. "Your face is all screwed up."

"I'm thinking."

"About what?"

"About how exactly to up the tension in this novel." Madeleine took the time to explain as Hugh sometimes had good ideas. "I want to introduce some real action, but I don't want to write myself into a corner."

"How would you write yourself into a corner?"

"Well, I don't know who the murderer is yet, so I'm not sure what the motivation for this will be."

"I wouldn't worry about it," Hugh said. "There's always more than one motivation at play."

"I guess so."

"Write it, decide if it's a red herring or not later," Hugh advised. "You can always rewrite it to make it work."

Madeleine wrinkled her nose. She had never embraced the idea of going back, rewriting, though she knew that most writers did. She wrote chronologically and once the words were down they seemed immovable.

"How's Elmo?" Hugh grinned as he said the name. Among the many things about his wife's family that Dr. Hugh Lamond found amusing was his father-in-law's name. He rarely used it without smiling.

"Dad's put some kind of windmill in the garden—apparently it will run the fountains."

"We should have got married in that garden," Hugh replied.

Madeleine giggled. "God, can you imagine the photos? A bridal party of garden gnomes…"

Hugh loosened and pulled off his tie, draping it over the back of a chair. "I'll never understand why your father—"

"It's an ethnic thing, Hugh. More is always more, and as much as possible, even better."

"If I'd said that…"

"I'm allowed. I have inside knowledge." Madeleine closed the laptop. "Shall we have Jeeves rustle something up?"

"I have a practice meeting, I'm afraid. I only came home to change so it's just you and your writer-detective tonight."

"Oh." Madeleine's smile faded only a little. "An evening in front of the fire with Ned McGinnity sounds divine."

Hugh Lamond's brow rose. "Should I be jealous?"

"Yes."

• • ● • •

Once Hugh left, Madeleine microwaved a casserole—at least she hoped that's what it was. It was difficult to tell what exactly had been frozen in the Tupperware, but casserole was a reasonably educated guess. Bringing it back to the living room, she propped the steaming bowl of something on the bookshelf beside her writing chair. A hunt through the television stations yielded an old Agatha Christie she'd seen years before. A hazy memory of the film was enough to allow her to follow its plot without paying undue attention. It would keep her company, and from focussing too hard on her writing, but no more. And with Christie, she felt among friends.

She hesitated, aware that what she did now would set the course of the novel. Madeleine took a breath. Right. She was just going to have to risk it and trust that Edward McGinnity would do the rest. She closed her eyes, looking for where she'd find him.

He'd just arrived home. It was late. He didn't bother to turn on the lights, confident navigating his own home in the dark.

Edward dropped his car keys into the pewter receptacle on the sideboard. A metallic clatter confirmed the keys had found their place and he continued into the kitchen. He opened the refrigerator door and it was in the weak illumination of the light it cast that he noticed an unexpected shadow. He turned, but too late. The first blow caught him in the jaw and a forearm locked around his throat from behind, the hold tightening and choking as he struggled.

Edward's eyes had adjusted just enough to make out three figures—men. The one who had him in a head-lock had recently eaten a large amount of hummus, but beyond that he could distinguish little else.

Restrained, he could do nothing to defend him-self when the other two began to pound. They were workman-like, silent in the face of his demands, and then his pleas.

As Edward began to believe that this was how he would die, they stopped. Abruptly. They left him in a bloody heap on his own kitchen floor.

He could feel the tiles against his face. The refrigerator door was still open and by its light he saw a stray Matchbox car under the butcher's block. The Lamborghini. He'd wondered where that had gone, and for now it was something on which he could focus as he tried to replace the air that had been beaten from his lungs. The slam of the front door registered. Relief. Madeleine. She stared at him unsure, hand clasped over her mouth.

She seemed so real, so present. She shouldn't have been standing in his kitchen. Edward tried to ask her what she was doing there, but he couldn't get out all the words. Then his head swam again.

He reached for the phone in his breast pocket, hoping it hadn't been smashed in the attack, and called for help.

• • ● • •

Madeleine bit her lip, fixed on what she'd just put into train. The look on Edward's face as his eyes locked with hers. And his words.

"What are you doing?"

He'd looked so bewildered, reproachful. As if he knew she'd visited pain and violence upon him with no real idea as to why. She shifted uncomfortably, guilty, sorry that she'd hurt him…and ashamed. Did he consider it the sensationalist trick of a hack—gratuitous violence for cheap titillation?

Madeleine groaned. No! She was being ridiculous. Edward McGinnity wasn't real and even if he was, she knew her craft as he did his. She was writing a crime fiction with all the suspense and action the genre entailed. Who was he to judge her decisions?

But still, this was a big plot commitment. She had no idea who would want to attack Edward McGinnity and for what reason. At some point, she was going to have to make it tie in, or everything she wrote henceforth would be wasted. But for now, she couldn't deny that it increased the heartbeat of her story.

• • ● • •

It was Leith Henry whom Edward called. She came immediately and rang an ambulance and the police the moment she saw the state of him.

By the time the ambulance arrived she had him off the floor, on the couch, with makeshift icepacks made of tea towels and various packets of frozen vegetables. The attending paramedics insisted that he go to the hospital. His protest was too confused and weak to have any effect, and Leith was by that stage deciding for him and directing proceedings. And so, when the police pulled up, Edward McGinnity was already leaving in the back of an ambulance.

For Edward, the next couple of hours passed in a blur of bright lights and monitors and antiseptic smells. Aside from the pain, he felt blindsided. Three men had broken into his home and belted the living dickens out of him…that kind of thing just didn't happen. It was absurd. And yet, here he was at the hospital. A dislocated shoulder was set right, stitches above his left brow, and X-rays to identify three broken ribs. The hospital would keep him overnight at a minimum, and the police asked their questions from his bedside.

Edward could give them little. He could not identify his assailants, they had told him nothing and he could think of no reason why anyone would break into his home and try to break him.

Bourke was clearly sceptical. "Were they after information, Mr. McGinnity? Did they ask you anything?"

"No."

"Could you perhaps have something they want?"

"If I do, they didn't ask me for it. I'm telling you, Detective, they didn't say a word."

"Do you have any enemies, Mr. McGinnity?"

"Enemies? No."

Bourke flicked through his notebook. "We have a complaint from a Mr. Elliot Kaufman. He alleges that you assaulted him."

"Does he?"

"Did you?"

"We had a disagreement." Edward winced as he sat up. "It wasn't a big deal."

"He seems to think it was."

"He'd hardly make a complaint and have me beaten up…even he's not that stupid."

"Would you care to tell us the nature of your disagreement with Mr. Kaufman?"

"No."

Bourke waited.

"Kaufman is married to a friend of mine. Sometimes I don't believe he shows her the respect he should."

"And your friend is Ms. Meriwether?"

"Yes."

"Is there anywhere you can stay for a couple of nights, Mr. McGinnity?"

"You think they'll come back?"

Bourke shrugged. "Our people are still going over the scene."

"You're going through my house. Don't you need a warrant or something—?"

"It's a crime scene, Mr. McGinnity. We're searching for evidence of your attackers."

Edward fell back, closing his eyes against the fluorescent lights of the hospital. A throbbing tenderness with a periodic pulse of white blinding pain. "Fine, just hurry up. I'm going home tomorrow."

A doctor came in then with Leith Henry in his wake. He called the interview to an end as he checked the chart at the foot of Edward's hospital bed with an air of concern. He maintained this semblance of an impending medical emergency until the policemen had left. And then he told Edward to get some rest and departed.

Madeleine smiled. Leith was in charge, even here.

The agent took the chair beside the bed. "Do you want to tell me what happened, Ned?"

He opened his eyes and looked at her. "I wasn't hiding anything, Leith. I have no idea who they were or what they wanted."

She sighed. "Maybe you'll think of something later. Right now we need to worry about where you're going to live."

"I have a house," Edward said. "How long can it take to dust for prints or whatever it is they're doing?"

Leith frowned. "I'm not sure it's safe for you to go back…after what happened."

For a moment Edward said nothing. "I'll get a security system," he offered in the end.

Leith shook her head.

"And a dog…I'm not going to be chased out of my house."

"That's very masculine, Ned, and very stupid."

He groaned.

Leith stopped. "Are you in pain, Ned? Should I call a doctor?"

"Yes, but no. I'll be fine. I don't suppose you could get me a coffee?"

"We haven't finished talking about this!" Leith grabbed her handbag and prepared to find a cafeteria or at least a vending machine. "This is serious, Ned, and as much as dying might help your sales, I'd rather you were alive to write sequels."

He laughed, grimacing and clutching his ribcage as he did so. "Only genre writers do sequels, Leith."

"Don't be a snob, Ned." She paused at the doorway. "We'll talk about your living arrangements when I return."

• • ● • •

Edward eased himself into the armchair by the window. He could hear Mrs. Jesmond in the kitchen. Though Leith had arranged for professional cleaners to come in once the police had finished, the housekeeper had scrubbed every square inch of the kitchen, using bleach on the tiles where blood had stained the grout. She was baking now, determined that danger could not co-exist with the warm sweet aroma of jam drops in the oven. Perhaps she was right. The incident seemed more a dream now, but for the bruised ache of his body.

A new security system had been installed while he was in the hospital. It had gone off twice that morning, triggered by a neighbourhood cat and then Leith herself when she'd arrived to check he'd memorised the passwords properly.

Edward uncapped his pen. He hadn't been able to write or even think about what he would write in the past couple of days. There was no space in hospital, where every conscious moment was crowded with nurses and visitors and incessantly beeping machines, and unconsciousness was monitored and disturbed.

His memory of the assault was broken—jagged disjointed sensations, but he did remember that Madeleine was there. Perhaps that was strange—he wasn't sure. Why would he think of her then? Was it because she was a crime-writer? God, in a moment of weakness had he fallen into some hackneyed platitude of life imitating art?

Or was it something more complex than that? He hoped it was. For some reason this manuscript, this process, felt different. He was intrigued more than puzzled by the change…and quietly excited.

Mrs. Jesmond came in with a tray—tea, biscuits, nervous comfort. The heightened flush of her face was noticeable in a frame of over-bleached hair. She fussed over him. "Shall I get you a pillow? Are you warm enough, Edward?"

He sensed something. "Mrs. Jesmond, is something bothering you?"

She stopped, rubbing her hands up and down the skirt of her apron. Twice she started, but no words came. And then, "I can't stay. You'll have to find someone else…I'm so sorry."

Edward asked her to sit, and tried to pour her a cup of tea. She took the pot from him and poured the cups herself. "You really shouldn't use that arm, darlin'. Not until your shoulder is healed."

"Do you feel unsafe here, Mrs. Jesmond?"

"It's not me as much as my Burt. He says it's too dangerous."

"Yes, of course he would." Edward took a deep sip of tea. "I can't ask you to come here if you or Mr. Jesmond feel at all uneasy."

"But what will you do?"

"I'm a grown man, Mrs. Jesmond."

At this she smiled.

He smiled too. "I'll hire another housekeeper, just until you're ready to come back."

"I'm not sure Burt will ever be ready, darlin'. And when I think of what happened in my kitchen…"

"We can deal with that as we come to it. Let's just say you're taking a leave of absence for now. I'll keep paying your salary, of course. Please, just don't take another job until you're absolutely sure."

Mrs. Jesmond's glasses fogged and she removed them, blinking furiously. "I feel so bad…to leave you on your own."

"I'm not on my own," Edward said without thinking. Of course, he was. "Anyway, until the police find these men, I'd be happier knowing you're not going to be dragged into it."

"Do they have any idea who…?"

He shook his head. He really didn't want to alarm her any further, but he told her the truth. "They didn't take anything…that I've noticed, anyway. Bourke thinks it may have been some sort of professional hit. They wore gloves except for when they…well, they didn't leave any prints. In fact, aside from what they did in the kitchen, they were surprisingly neat."

Mrs. Jesmond stared at her hands, inspecting a chip in the pearlescent polish. "How will you manage? That hospital should have kept you…the way they shuffle people out these days…"

"I'm not sick. I just have to take it easy for a couple of days." Edward was touched by her distress, her vacillation on his account. He didn't mention that the police believed that his attackers might have already been in the house waiting, when she'd come in to clean. He leaned forward gingerly and patted her hand. "I plan to hole up and write anyway, so having a reason to turn down invitations to go out and procrastinate is probably a good thing."

"I'll make sure the ice-box is well stocked," she said quite tearfully now. "You'll just have to reheat what you want, for a while at least."

"I can always call out for pizza," he said smiling.

"Promise me you won't, Edward!" The housekeeper stood, straightening her narrow shoulders and thrusting out her chest. "Nothing would upset me more than the thought that I had left you to survive on pizza and beer like some...some..." Mrs. Jesmond faltered, unable to think of who would be so unfortunate.

Edward laughed. He suddenly felt like pizza.

Damage

"Have you worked out who attacked me?" Edward asked. Madeleine d'Leon was wearing blue pyjamas with some kind of cloud print. She sat cross-legged in an old armchair with her laptop perched on a cushion in her lap. He was startled when she looked up.

"I'm sorry. It's the story. It's not like the stuff you write—something's actually got to happen."

"Things happen in my work," he said, mildly affronted. "They're just more subtle than beating someone up physically."

"Sure."

"The demons of our own creation are always more dangerous than the ones who walk through the door, Maddie. And the struggle more interesting."

She rolled her eyes and laughed at him. "Yes, of course, the inner journey. Worthy navel-gazing. I just write stories, Ned."

He laughed too. If only she knew.

Madeleine slipped back to focus on what she was doing. She checked her watch. This was the third practice meeting Hugh had attended in a week. It was past midnight. He'd never been this late before.

She closed the laptop and took the cold grey remains of her casserole into the kitchen. She switched the kettle on more out of absent habit than anything else and glanced out of the window in search of headlights on the road. Just darkness. Perhaps Hugh was having car trouble. She hated the idea of being one of those people who constantly rang their partner, but perhaps he was having car trouble. So she rang. A recorded voice told her the phone was out of range. That was odd.

Madeleine wondered whether she should ring Hugh's nurse…but that would sound clingy, like she was checking up on him. But what if he was having car trouble and the phone was malfunctioning? Perhaps she should drive into Ashwood herself. Yes, that was the thing to do.

She pulled on jeans and a cotton jumper, boots without bothering with socks, and then coaxed the old Mercedes out of the driveway, all the time hoping that Hugh would arrive home. Now that she'd decided to do something, his absence seemed more ominous and she felt a fluttering of panic. What if it was more than simple car trouble?

The headlights illuminated about twenty metres of country road before her. The dense scrub on both sides of the road made it darker than night, but she knew the way well enough to guess where the potholes lay and where the road's edge had been eroded away. When Madeleine saw the headlights coming towards her, she dipped her own lights and leaned forward trying to make out whether the oncoming car was Hugh's.

They must have jumped across in that brief moment when the beams of both vehicles lowered. Madeleine saw them only a gasp before impact. She closed her eyes as she slammed the brake pedal to the floor and yet she saw the kangaroo bounce onto the bonnet and slide towards her windscreen. A second thump then on the left, and a rattle that continued until she brought the car to a stop.

Madeleine climbed out and ran back. The other vehicle too, had stopped and returned to the point of collision. It was in its headlights that she saw the kangaroos. One dead, the other twisted, its powerful hind legs motionless as it tried to drag itself away with its forelimbs. It didn't make a sound, just looked at her with dark liquid eyes.

Madeleine stood staring, desperate for something, anything she could do.

A man and a woman climbed out of the utility. The Johnsons…neighbours or thereabouts.

"Are you all right, Maddie?"

Madeleine nodded, unable to take her eyes from the dying creature before her. God, if she could comfort it. She cried, knowing it was worse than useless, but unable to stop.

Keith Johnson glanced at his wife. "I'll duck home and get the gun."

"You're going to shoot it?" Madeleine sobbed, horrified. "Can't we…?"

"Its back is broken Maddie, and the poor bloody creature is in pain. A bullet is the kindest thing we could do."

Madeleine wept agreement. She knew he was right… but she'd done this.

• ● ● ● •

Edward put down the pen. His hand was shaking too violently to write. A lingering injury. Unrelated to the ones he'd sustained more recently.

God, his little brother, Jacob. Again. Before him. Alive. Trapped. Dying. That same bewildered fear in his eyes, the same instinctive need to crawl away.

Edward gasped; his chest hurt.

Somehow he'd written the accident into every book…without meaning to, without wanting to…but it was always there. Jacob had been alive for such a little while. He hadn't made a sound and yet Edward could hear him screaming even now. Edward swallowed as he saw what he'd done. He'd put his little brother into a broken kangaroo. What was wrong with him, for God's sake? Why couldn't he leave it be?

Keith Johnson was back quickly. Madeleine turned away as he put down the injured beast. One shot, louder than she expected. The rest passed indistinctly…once the tow truck had collected her car, the Johnsons drove her home.

Madeleine was grateful. Embarrassed and beset by such a keen regret. And still a little stunned. She was unsure what she would have done if the Johnsons hadn't stopped. And she barely knew them, though Hugh had delivered their son and treated them for all manner of lesser things. They spoke highly of him and warmly to him when they dropped her off.

"Where the hell were you going at this time of night?" Hugh asked as the Johnsons pulled away.

"Just into town."

"Why?"

"I thought you might have broken down."

"Why would you think that?"

"You didn't come home."

"Yes, I did. I'm here aren't I?"

"Hugh, it's three in the morning! You weren't answering your phone."

"I'm a doctor, Maddie…there was an emergency."

"You could have called."

"You know what I do. Why would you assume it was anything other than the usual crap?"

"Because I was worried and I couldn't reach you!" Madeleine was shouting now.

"You're being ridiculous, Maddie. I don't appreciate you trying to check up on me. It's quite insulting, to be honest."

Madeleine stared at him startled. "That's not what I was doing."

"I have to be up in the morning," he said. "I'll ring the insurance company about your car tomorrow."

They resorted to silence after that. Madeleine opened her laptop, putting the screen between her and Hugh. She pretended to write. He went to bed. In time, when she could keep her eyes open no longer, she slipped silently into that bed, lying rigidly on the far edge of her side. And she dreamt of Edward McGinnity.

"Are you all right?" her writer asked. For a moment she simply savoured the image of him. He looked at her from within her and suddenly she felt shy.

"Yes. It's just a fight. People fight. I shouldn't have gone looking for him…that poor kangaroo…"

"That wasn't your fault. Sometimes things just happen. Are you sure you're okay? It was one heck of a collision."

Madeleine bit her lip, realising then how much she had wanted Hugh to say just that.

"I'm fine…Mercedes Benz…crumple zones." She tilted her head to one side considering the bruises on

Edward's face, the stitches. "It's not like I was beaten up by three unknown men."

He groaned. "Crime-writers! Obsessed with guns and masked bandits. There are other ways to make a point."

"There was no point to this," she said shaking her head. "It was just an accident. Irrelevant, unless it gave me an alibi…"

"I don't write crime fiction; I deal in the consequences of ordinary things."

"Sounds dull."

"Well, that depends on the reader, I guess."

Madeleine smiled. "I guess."

"I'm sorry. I know this is hard for you."

"What do you mean?" Madeleine bristled. She would not be condescended to. "I have five books to my name—I've done this before."

"I wasn't talking about what you're writing."

"I'm not sure what you're talking about," she sighed. "But I guess that's a literary tradition in itself."

"Comprehensibility is very genre," he replied gravely.

Madeleine laughed out loud. Hugh stirred and she smothered it.

• • ● • •

Willow was furious. She stormed into the house, slamming the door behind her and calling his name. Her eyes were bright and every punctuated movement articulated her outrage. "Ned. Ned! Where the hell are you?"

"Willow." Edward stood, using the back of his armchair for support as he straightened.

For a moment she wavered and then taking a deep

breath she launched. "You told the police that Elliot did this!"

"What?"

She marched up to him. "Sit down, I want to shout at you."

"I think I'll stand for that."

"How could you, Ned? Elliot is my husband!"

"I don't know what you think I told the police."

"They're questioning Elliot about your attack because you hit him! How is that fair?"

"I don't know. I didn't tell them to question Elliot."

"But you did hit him."

"Yeah, I did that."

"Why would you—how could you, Ned?"

Edward shrugged. "He told the police, not me, Will."

Willow sat down on the coffee table, clenching her hands in her hair. "Oh, God! What else could go wrong?"

"Andy flew in this morning. He'll be here in a couple of hours," Edward offered.

"Elliot and I look like Bonnie and Clyde now."

"Stay, speak to Andy."

She looked at him. Her face softened. "Are you all right, Ned? I wanted to come to the hospital, but Elliot…"

"I'm fine, a little sore, that's all."

"Do you have any idea…?"

"No. One of them had garlic breath but that's hardly an identikit."

"Poor darling." Willow forgot that she'd been angry with him. "Sit down. Can I get you anything?" She looked towards the kitchen. "It sounds like Mrs. Jesmond is cooking for thirty people."

"I suspect she's making sure I'll have enough home cooking to get me through while she's away."

"Where's she going?"

Edward lowered his voice. "What happened unnerved her a bit. I'm hoping she'll come back as soon as the police have arrested somebody."

"But that could take…what will you do?"

"I'm not a child, Will. I can look after myself."

"Why don't you come and stay with us?"

Edward laughed, clutching his chest as he was reminded of his fractured ribs. "Are you insane? You want me to stay with you and Elliot?" He pointed to the dark reflective hemisphere on the ceiling. "I'll be fine. Leith's had some kind of super security system installed."

Willow squinted. "Is that a camera?"

"Yes."

Her brow rose. "Is there one in your bedroom?"

Edward chuckled. "Of course you would ask that."

"Is there?"

"Yes. If you want to kill me and get away with it you'll have to do it in one of the bathrooms."

"Doesn't it bother you?" Willow glanced back at the camera uncomfortably. "It's like being on reality television."

"I don't plan to be doing much other than writing, and I'm not sure 'Author Idol' would be a ratings success," he said, though he was by no means comfortable with the idea.

Willow giggled. "I can just see viewers tuning in to find out exactly which adjective you chose."

"I intend to go out as much as possible," Edward admitted.

Willow leaned across to place her hand on his arm. "Aren't you the least bit scared, Ned?"

"Scared?"

She sighed. "Okay, let's say worried. Those men broke in here and waited for you with no other purpose than to beat the hell out of you."

"It wasn't personal, Will. They weren't angry, just efficient. I expect they were hired thugs."

"Why would that make you feel any safer?"

"Well, because they've done their job. If they'd wanted to kill me, they could easily have done so...so whoever hired them didn't tick that box on the order form."

"Why would someone want to simply give you a hiding?"

"Interesting question...they must have had a reason. We just need to figure out what that was."

Willow's eyes became sharp. "You're spending too much time with that crime-writer of yours, my darling. She's making you think you're Sherlock Holmes!"

Edward sat back. He did wonder how Madeleine would handle this. Would she see something he was missing? Why did people attack perfect strangers? She'd probably written a similar scenario at one time or another.

Willow stood and kissed him softly on the cheek. "I'm sorry you were hurt, Ned. And I'm sorry I didn't come to the hospital."

Edward met her eye. "I'm not sorry I hit Elliot, Will."

She said nothing for a moment, and then she spoke slowly and precisely, each word a declaration.

"I married Elliot. You're my best friend, Ned, but I love Elliot."

"Yes, I know."

"You're not allowed to hit him."

"What—never?"

"Oh, Ned!"

"Okay, yes, I know."

"And Elliot didn't have anything to do with the attack on you."

"I never thought he did."

Willow caught her hair back and twisted it. It sprang back when she let go. She twirled a tress distractedly around her finger. Edward had seen that before, when she was upset.

"I wish you and Elliot could get along," she said. "I don't understand how the two people I love most in the world could hate each other so much."

"You're clearly making a mistake with one of us."

"Ned…"

He smiled. "I'll try, okay."

• • ● • •

Hugh brought home flowers. A cheerful bouquet of gerberas and hothouse roses in clear cellophane and tissue. Madeleine inhaled the thin fragrance and allowed him to kiss her. So the fight was officially over.

One of Hugh Lamond's patients had mentioned that the kangaroos were particularly bad on the roads this year. "Apparently there's a gadget you can get for your car that will repel wildlife. I'll look into it when your car gets back from the smash repairers."

"Thank you." Madeleine smiled though she felt thwarted, denied the right to feel the resentment that now surged strongly in her breast. The flowers were a gag of sorts. They declared that any continuance of hostilities would be her doing and not his. She wanted to be angry—she wasn't finished being angry.

But she found a vase for the flowers anyway, enquired about his day, and empathised and sympathised as they cooked dinner. They talked of ordinary things, interest rates on their mortgage, investments, having the carpets dry-cleaned, updating wills—that sort of thing. He showed her the power of attorney documents he'd finally got back from the lawyer he'd hired. He'd already signed one set in the presence of the requisite witnesses, granting her power over his body and his property in the event he became incapacitated. The conversation was wary, too polite and Madeleine was aware of a fermenting panic in the pit of her stomach. The pasta they cooked tasted sour and it might not have been the fault of the sauce.

Hugh had another meeting that evening. Once again it was midnight and he hadn't returned. Madeleine wondered whether he was testing her, daring her to check up on him. When had they started doing that to each other? She didn't try to ring him or even listen for the phone. Instead she once again fell asleep on a damp pillow.

Old Allies

Andy Finlay had come straight from the airport. His silk tie bore the stains of an inflight culinary mishap…a portion which proved ill-suited to plastic cutlery. He might not have minded if the meal had been worth eating. As it was, the tie had been sacrificed for naught.

The lawyer shook Edward McGinnity's hand warmly. "How are you, Ned?" he asked, scrutinising the young man's face, assessing and cataloguing each bruise with a litigator's eye.

Edward grinned. "The police haven't identified anyone for you to sue, Andy."

"In that case, I'm glad you're out of the hospital. Ms. Meriwether—how are you, my dear?"

Willow stepped out from behind Edward and shook Finlay's hand. "I'm afraid I need your help, Mr. Finlay."

"Don't be afraid, Ms. Meriwether. Ned here, has asked me to represent you and I'm rather good at what I do." He turned back to Edward. "Why don't I speak to Ms. Meriwether in your study, Ned?"

Edward nodded. He was being dismissed so that Finlay could speak to his new client alone. "I'll have Mrs. Jesmond bring you some coffee."

"Good boy." Finlay placed his hand on Edward's shoulder, the gesture light, a casual, barely noticeable familiarity. "We can have a drink later. Turning towards the study, he said "After you, Ms. Meriwether."

"Andy…" Edward pulled him aside. "You'll look after Willow—?"

"Ned." Finlay raised his hand. "I assure you that once Ms. Meriwether is my client, then her interests are all I'll be looking after. You know that."

"Yes, sorry."

"Now I have one question for you." Finlay's grey eyes narrowed under the unruly upsweep of his brows. "Is there any chance that Ms. Meriwether's interests will run counter to yours?"

"Mine? No, of course not."

"Because once I accept her as a client, it's her interests and only hers that I can consider."

"Good. This has nothing to do with me, Andy."

"And this?" Finlay moved his gaze to the stitches on Edward's face.

Edward wondered how much his old guardian already knew. "Not related, Andy. I presume I disturbed a burglary."

"Hmmm." Finlay did not seem convinced. "You are aware, aren't you, Ned, that if I represent Ms. Meriwether, I may not be able to represent you should the need arise?"

"It won't. The need won't arise."

Finlay sighed. "Very well." He turned abruptly back towards the study, humming "Bohemian Rhapsody."

● ● ● ● ●

Edward put his hand up against the brightness of the
studio lights.

"Sorry about that, Ned. I'll adjust it in just a tick."
Jason Henry fiddled with the angle of the lamp. "Leith
wants me to make sure we can see the stitches clearly."

"Where is she?"

"Making tea, seeing as you no longer have staff."

Jason was Leith Henry's husband, a filmmaker of
some acclaim in the world of art-house films. Slim, wiry,
his every movement spoke of energy, he dressed like a
modern beatnik, though he looked like he'd slept in his
clothes. He was here to conduct his biannual interview
with Edward McGinnity. The idea was some mad notion
of Leith's—an archive of candid temporal interviews
which would be the basis of a biographical film once
Edward became renowned enough for anyone to care
about what mattered to him when he was still unknown.
Edward thought the idea ludicrous, but it was easier to
subject himself to an on-camera interview twice a year
than to say no to Leith. He was reasonably confident
that the footage would never see the light of day.

"Cup of tea, pet?" Leith chirped, coming in with a
tray.

"That'd be nice, love," Jason replied.

"Coming up, pet."

"You're a keeper, love."

Edward said nothing initially, choosing not to inter-
rupt the exchange of endearments which had never
ceased to amuse the Henries. They had petted and
loved each other through ten years and three children…
clearly the words had some magic. He was willing to
wait, within reason.

But then reason became stretched.

"I try my best, pet—"

"Would you just pour the flaming tea?" Edward snarled. "Pet or love or whoever you are…"

Leith beamed at him. "Of course, pet. Extra sugar for you!"

The incidents of the last few days had not persuaded Leith to postpone the latest instalment of filming. Indeed, she was particularly eager to "capture" the drama. "A physical skirmish makes a change from your more esoteric struggles," she'd said when he questioned it. "Perhaps we should put your arm in a sling for the interview."

"No."

"Don't worry, I can put it in with the editing software." Jason hunched over the camera in his fashion, as if he intended to devour the image. "We could put a cast on his leg, too, if you want."

Edward assumed quite hopefully that he was kidding.

"So, Ned, tell us about this bloke who was murdered."

"Geoffrey Vogel. He was a critic."

"An art critic."

"No. I believe he was happy to pass judgement on just about anything. He wrote a column for the *Herald*."

"How'd he die, then?"

"Broke his neck falling down the fire stairs."

"Bad business."

"For him, I guess. I don't think it's a great loss."

"We might need to edit that out." Leith tapped her husband. "It makes him sound a bit unfeeling."

"You're filming?" Edward pulled up, alarmed.

It occurred to Madeleine then that the footage could be used against Edward. Perhaps that's what she'd been setting up. Her mind didn't always tell her what it was planning. She put the idea away for later.

Knowing now that the camera was recording, Edward became more circumspect. Jason peppered him with questions for more than an hour, interrogating him about the assault, and all that led up to it and of course his writing. Edward responded honestly, but often quite flippantly. Leith watched on with her arms folded.

"Okay," Jason said finally. "I think I've got enough. By the time I'm finished, writing books will sound like an extreme sport!"

"Fabulous!" Leith rewarded him with another cup of tea. "You do your magic and I'll get it to the media guys."

"Media guys?" Edward frowned. "What's going on?"

"I've had some media interest in you, Ned. It could help build you a platform."

"A platform? What are you talking about?"

"*Limelight* wants to do a piece on you."

Edward groaned. He'd watched *Limelight*. The show purported to do biographical pieces, documentaries about the lives of celebrities. But though its production values were excellent and its following massive, *Limelight* did have a tabloid quality to it. "You can't be serious, Leith…"

She sat down next to him, and delivered a prepared placation. "We've just shot the interview, Ned. It's the only reason I'm considering it. We have editorial control. It'll be excellent publicity."

"I'm not that kind of writer, Leith."

"You mean the kind that sells books?"

"No, it's—"

"A wonderful opportunity. Barn Owl has great hopes for *Sentience*. We have to do our bit."

"I don't think this is a good idea." Edward stood, suddenly needing to get out of shot.

"Look, Ned, *Limelight* was going to do a story on you, anyway. Our cooperation means we can frame the angle, rather than leaving it to some scandal-hungry journalist."

"Why? Why do they suddenly want to do a story on me?"

Leith shrugged. "The producer of *Limelight* is related to the fiction editor at Barn Owl. I expect your name came up at some family dinner. It's how it works—where are you going?"

"I need a drink."

"Ned, trust me. It'll be fine."

Madeleine murmured sympathetically as she wrote. She'd been so flattered and excited when the media first showed interest. Her own publicist had arranged for her to appear on *A Word in the Hand*, a kind of televised book club. It seemed so glamorous then. Hair, makeup, autographs. Of course she'd since come to understand the reluctance Edward felt. It was difficult for a writer to succeed in the public eye. To those who hated your work, you were an undeserving hack; to those who loved it, you rarely lived up. Good writers were not as interesting as their characters. That probably wasn't surprising.

But Leith was quite determined. She tried guilt. "You're asking people for the privilege of entering their heads, of guiding their imaginations for a time. It's only natural they want to know who you are."

"My books aren't about me, Leith."

"Of course they are…all books are about the writer. Look, Ned, what's amazing about your work is the intimacy you establish with your reader. They hear your voice, they trust it, they allow you to break their hearts and make them anew. The very least you owe them is the occasional interview."

"Give in, mate," Jason Henry advised. "Don't make her hurt you. She will, if she has to."

Edward sighed, turning back towards his agent. "I don't suppose you had anything to do with the three men who—?"

"Edward McGinnity, how could you suggest such a thing?" Leith's hands went to her hips and her nostrils flared. "*I* wouldn't have let them touch your face… Barn Owl wants new author photos." She frowned as she assessed the situation. "You're going to look like you write crime."

• • ● • •

Madeleine considered ignoring the knock but she suspected that she'd been seen. That was quickly confirmed.

"Maddie, I know you're in there! Answer the door—it's only me."

Madeleine saved her work and closed the laptop. Lillian wouldn't leave in a hurry. There was no point pretending she'd get back to the manuscript that morning.

"I'm not going away!"

Madeleine opened the door and smiled at the strong-bodied woman who stood on her threshold. Lillian's stance was wide and immovable, braced as though she expected Madeleine to try and push her off the step.

"Hello, Lil, what are you doing here?"

"Making sure you don't turn into a complete hermit. Get dressed—we're going shopping."

"I was working." Madeleine could hear the whine in her own voice.

"Don't care. You've been doing nothing but working for ages." She glanced disdainfully at the blue cloud print pyjamas. "You need some new clothes…you're letting yourself go, girl."

"I'm a writer. Nobody cares what I look like."

"You have a husband." Lillian followed Madeleine into the house. "And, personally, I'm over this boudoir chic look of yours. Come on, we'll go into Hampton, buy clothes, drink decent coffee, make sure the bookshops have the latest Madeleine d'Leon novel."

"I really wanted to finish—"

"For God's sake, Maddie, you're too old to spend all your time with imaginary friends. I'm sure Veronica Killwilly can spare you for a few hours."

Madeleine groaned defeat. "Okay, give me a second to get dressed." She didn't mention that she was not working on another Veronica Killwilly novel. She wasn't sure why. Usually she loved talking about her work, testing ideas, telling the story. In some ways she needed to tell before she could write. But not this time. Now she was aware only of a vague need to satisfy Lillian as quickly as possible so she could get back to Edward.

Madeleine pulled a shirt over her head, reproaching herself for her reluctance. It was disloyal. Lillian was her friend, a good friend. She helped her prepare query letters for dozens of agents when her first manuscript was newborn. She brought champagne and ice cream to celebrate when Leith Henry had replied—they'd mixed them together and toasted literature with frothy cocktails. And she'd been to every one of Madeleine's book launches, dressed up as Veronica Killwilly like some deranged fan.

Madeleine grabbed her bag and joined Lillian in the hallway. At the last moment she remembered the documents granting Hugh her power of attorney in the event of incapacity, which were still awaiting execution. She had Lillian witness her signature and left the legal papers on the dining room table, pleased that she'd managed to complete at least one of the chores of real life which were so often neglected when she wrote. "Right, then, let's shop. Actually, I could use some new pyjamas."

Lillian shoved her. "Honey, you do realise that you've started dressing like you live in a nursing home? It's not normal, dude."

"I've become pyjama-shaped, Lil."

Lillian studied her. "Perhaps we can stop the rot before it goes too far."

Edward studied Madeleine too. He couldn't see any rot at all. There was a softness about her figure, but he didn't think that a bad thing by any means. She was not a literary writer after all.

Hampton was about a ninety-minutes' drive from Ashwood. A major centre for a number of smaller towns, it boasted a central business district which served several times its own population, and included specialist outlets and department stores. Once upon a time, before she began writing, Madeleine had shopped there once a week. She'd loved wandering, stopping for coffee, taking in the occasional movie. But now those old pleasures were compromised by a restlessness to return to other worlds.

Still, Lillian's company was a tonic. At the heart of their relationship was the fact that they could make each other laugh, the kind of hysterical giggling laughter that left them stumbling and intoxicated, that fed on itself so that everything was suddenly funny. It was like a blast that put the tension and strain of the past days into sharp relief.

Lillian dragged her into fashion boutiques and insisted she try on real clothes.

"I don't really wear skirts anymore," Madeleine protested as Lillian handed her a dress.

"What about work?"

"I have enough suits. Board meetings are only once a month."

"No, I meant for your writer stuff. Don't you have a festival in a couple of weeks?"

Madeleine grimaced. "I never wear skirts on panels."

"Whyever not? This one's really pretty."

Madeleine sighed. "I just can't talk intelligently and sit like a lady at the same time…it's safer to wear jeans."

"You're kidding?"

"Sadly not…I've never been able to cross my legs without tipping over."

Lillian was giggling again. "We might need to sign you up for some yoga classes."

"Or I could just wear jeans."

"I can't believe writers worry about stuff like that."

"We don't worry…we just wear jeans."

"Come on." Lillian checked her watch. "Coffee stop."

They found a table at Scribbles, so called for the butchers'-paper tablecloths and crayons on every table. The work of the students at the Hampton School of Art was displayed on its walls for sale as well as inspiration. Lillian took the red crayon and began to draw what looked like a hamburger.

"So," she said, "suppose you tell me what's made you so unavailable lately. If I didn't know better, I'd think you were having an affair."

Madeleine laughed.

"So what gives then?"

"I'm just working, Lil. I've only got a couple of months to finish this book."

"You need to be more assertive, Maddie. Tell them they'll get the next Veronica Killwilly when you finish writing it and if that takes a year, well they'll just have to wait!"

"I can't see that going well, I'm afraid." Madeleine did not correct Lillian's assumption that she was writing another Veronica Killwilly.

"Don't you have an agent? Can't you get her to tell them to back off?"

"It's not really the publishers, Lil, it's me. I like writing. I want to finish…" Madeleine trailed off, jarred by her own words. She didn't want to finish the book at all. The very thought of finishing with Edward McGinnity made her feel panicked, and bereft. "I want to write."

"All the time?"

"A lot of it. I'm sorry. I know it sounds mad. I just get—"

"Obsessed?"

"Focussed."

Lillian smiled, though there was a sharpness in it, a flash of something—hurt, or perhaps irritation.

"I suppose that's what it takes to be a writer. You've got to be willing to make the sacrifices. I've always cared too much about my family and friends."

"I do care. I don't know how to explain it. I just have to write. It's like I'm only completely me when I'm writing."

"You didn't always write. Were you not you then?"

"Not completely."

Lillian laughed. But scorn was cut into the mirth like some bitter essence folded into whipped cream. "Who was it that married Hugh, then? Some kind of half-you? You're being ridiculous, Maddie."

The words cut, and for a moment Madeleine simply bled. "I didn't mean—"

"You know, Maddie, perhaps you should occasionally take stock of how good you have it. There are dozens of women who'd give anything to be married to Hugh Lamond."

Madeleine wasn't sure how to respond. The censure seemed to come from nowhere, and she'd been unprepared. How had this become about her and Hugh? "Has Hugh said something?"

Lillian took a deep breath. "No. Of course not. I just think you should be fair."

"Hugh works as hard as I do, Lil."

"Yes, but he's a doctor. He actually earns real money and he's saving lives. I love your books, Maddie, I do, but they're just stories. No one's going to live or die."

Madeleine said nothing, sealing in the rage behind tightly pressed lips. Inside, a jumbled spitting fury was contained, though the flash was visible in her eyes. Her own words were being used against her and she had no defence. How often had she derided the self-importance of literature?

Edward watched, nodding unconsciously, as he felt the outrage in Madeleine's breast, the professional pride she was so fond of denying. It was time for her to stop hiding behind a determination not to take herself too seriously. Risk came with taking yourself seriously and her best work would come out of that vulnerability.

Evidence

Madeleine shut the door behind her, leaning back against it as she listened for Lillian's car pulling out. The ride back from Hampton had been an exhausting journey of forced congeniality, tinny laughter that died in her throat and a frost that settled like a shroud over a friendship that had just that morning been warm and vibrant. She was still too livid to grieve the demise.

She made tea, muttering to herself. Every past irritation with Lillian was resurrected, sharpened and nailed into the coffin.

Frustrated tears. She wanted to write, but she was too angry, clenched. She sat down with the computer nevertheless. How dare Lillian! Who did she think she was? Hugh did not need her to advocate on his behalf. It was six o'clock. He would probably not be home for hours yet.

Madeleine wiped her eyes to focus properly on the screen, to read over what she last wrote and to think about something other than her own life, about which she had no right to complain. Lillian's words…"dozens of women who'd give anything to be married to Hugh

Lamond." Who did she mean? Was Lillian trying to warn her? For the first time she wondered why Hugh would think she'd been checking up on him. Why he'd been so angry…why he was now so distant.

She forced her mind back to Edward. He wouldn't treat Willow like that.

"I wouldn't treat *you* like that." Edward replaced the cap on his pen.

"You don't know me." Madeleine smiled at herself. "Willow's the love of your life. I'm just a writer."

"Just?"

"Yes, just. I tell stories, that's all."

"Do you need to do more?"

"I don't know."

"Do you want to do more?"

"No. I don't."

He was close to her now. She might have touched him if she reached out. She closed her eyes and allowed herself to brush his hand with hers; quickly, as if the contact might burn, or worse. Edward smiled at her, still, reassuring, amused by her uncertainty.

Madeleine pulled back, a little shocked. She'd felt something of substance, she was sure. A pressure and a warmth against her fingers. It should have frightened her but instead she was strangely elated…and curious.

Was she stepping through the looking glass, she wondered. Would she be able to step back? Was this just a moment of indulgence, of madness, or something more?

Madeleine shook her head and returned to the laptop, to her story where Edward McGinnity actually belonged.

• • ● • •

Bourke set off the security alarm, and so he and his colleagues were admitted in a flurry of code-punching panic as Edward disarmed the system.

"Detective Bourke," Edward said when the sirens had finally been silenced. "Good morning."

Bourke nodded. And then he served his warrant.

"You want to search my house again?" Edward stared at the document perplexed. "You searched it just a couple of days ago."

"We'd also like you to accompany us to the station, Mr. McGinnity. We have a few questions."

"About what?"

"We'll explain at the station."

"And if I refuse?"

"If you won't accompany us voluntarily, we'll be forced to arrest you."

"Arrest me? What the hell for?"

"For the murder of Geoffrey Vogel."

"You can't be serious."

"I am very serious, Mr. McGinnity."

Edward rubbed his shoulder absently as he contemplated resisting. There probably wasn't any point. "I need to make a phone call," he said in the end.

"You can do that at the station."

"Fine." Edward gave up. It was clear he didn't have a choice.

"We appreciate your cooperation, Mr. McGinnity."

"Always happy to volunteer, Detective," Edward replied curtly.

Madeleine's breath came evenly again now. This

was classic crime fiction—evidence, accusations, red herrings—this she understood.

• • ● • •

"The backseat, if you don't mind, McGinnity," Bourke said as Edward reached for the front passenger door of the police car.

Bourke's partner held the rear door open and waited for Edward to climb in. The car smelled of cigarette smoke and some kind of pine-scented air freshener that was not up to the task. Edward watched what seemed like an entire regiment of police officers file into his house as the police car reversed out of his driveway.

"Could you tell me what you're looking for, Detective?"

"Let's just wait till we're at the station, why don't we, Mr. McGinnity?" Bourke met Edward's eye in the rear-view mirror.

Edward shrugged, wincing as the movement caught his injured shoulder.

They gave him a moment to make a phone call in the sparsely furnished interview room. He stopped halfway through dialling Andy Finlay's number. Finlay was acting for Willow now. Edward didn't want to risk compromising that. But he didn't have another lawyer. He groaned. If only Madeleine d'Leon wasn't a figment of his imagination...of course her specialisation was corporate, but she did write crime. He took a deep breath clearing the ridiculous train of thought from his head, and he dialled the number of Leith Henry.

He told her briefly where he was and why.

She told him she'd be there with a lawyer within the hour.

Bourke returned, introducing the detective who accompanied him as O'Neil, before inviting Edward to sit. They offered him tea, which he declined, and then water, which he accepted.

"Right, Detective Bourke," Edward said. "Suppose you tell me what this is all about."

"Has Mr. Vogel ever been in your house, Mr. McGinnity?"

"Vogel…no. We weren't friends."

"Could he have been admitted when you were not there, by your housekeeper, perhaps?"

"No. Mrs. Jesmond doesn't let anyone in when I'm not at home. She's particular about that sort of thing."

"Does anybody else have a key to your residence?"

"My agent, Leith Henry."

"Might she have admitted Vogel?"

"No. She didn't like him either. She definitely wouldn't have let him into my house. What is this about?"

"We found traces of blood in—"

"Of course. I bled all over the kitchen a couple of days ago, if you recall."

"It wasn't your blood." Bourke glanced at his partner. "Can you think of any reason why we might have found traces of Mr. Vogel's blood in your house, sir?"

Stunned, Edward stared at the detectives.

O'Neil opened his notebook and flicked through it until he found the page he was looking for. "Traces of Mr. Vogel's blood were found in the sink of and on the shower door of the upstairs bathroom adjoining the master bedroom."

Again Edward said nothing.

"Can you tell us why Mr. Vogel's blood would be found in your bathroom, Mr. McGinnity?"

Edward shook his head. "No, I can't."

They asked him the same question again several times, in several different ways. They suggested that now would be the best time to confess, that perhaps it was an accident, a careless belligerence at the head of the fire stairs.

"No."

"I think Mr. Vogel's blood might have been transferred to you when you were trying to help him after the fall. Perhaps you checked his pulse."

"I didn't."

"Why didn't you check his pulse? Was it that obvious he was dead?"

"No—"

"So you didn't realise he was dead."

"No."

"Well, why didn't you call for help, an ambulance or—"

"I wasn't there!" Aware he'd raised his voice, Edward sat back, trying to regain his composure as the detectives drew conclusions from the fact that they'd rattled him.

Edward's head throbbed, and the light seemed bright and pounding. He fumbled inside his jacket and extracted a small canister of pills.

O'Neil moved quickly to take them from him.

"It's pain medication, Detective," Edward said wearily. "I was supposed to take a couple of pills about an hour ago."

Bourke checked the label. He stood. "I might just have this checked, to be safe."

"Fine," Edward said resigned.

Bourke returned without the pills, sitting down to continue the interview with only a vague explanation that the contents of the canister were being "verified."

"In the meantime, Mr. McGinnity, perhaps we could go over the events of the night Mr. Vogel was killed."

"Yes, fine," Edward said distractedly. His various injuries were competing for attention as the previous dose of painkillers wore off.

The detectives interrogated him about the night of Willow Meriwether's opening. The questions were aggressive, accusatory. Edward remained calm, batting back with denials, though increasingly preoccupied with the tightening band of pain around his temples and the tenderness of his ribs with every breath.

A constable came in and Bourke and O'Neil left with her, telling him they would not be long. When they returned, however, it was with Leith Henry and a man she declared to be Edward McGinnity's solicitor.

Edward stood to shake Ian Denholm's hand. The lawyer's grip was firm, his manner assured.

"Are you all right, Ned?" Leith studied Edward's face. "You look pale." She felt his forehead. "You're warm."

"I'm a bit late with the pills the hospital gave me."

"Well take them now!"

Edward glanced at Bourke. "The detective is having them checked."

Denholm turned to the policeman. "Am I to understand, Detective, that you deprived my client of his pain medication before questioning him without the presence of legal counsel?"

Bourke said nothing.

"I take it that since Mr. McGinnity does not appear to have been informed of his rights, he is not under arrest?"

"Mr. McGinnity is voluntarily helping us with enquiries."

Edward snorted.

Denholm's brows rose. One side of his mouth curved up, a lawyerly combination of satisfaction and contempt. "We'll be leaving now, Detectives. If you'd just return the medication my client was prescribed."

Bourke and O'Neil consulted briefly. Then Bourke stepped aside. "If you'll come this way?"

They went directly from the station to the city offices of Fitzgibbon Etheridge at which Ian Denholm was a partner. The lawyer's personal office was large but looked out upon the car park. The desk still had that brand new lustre, the upholstery that just-unwrapped smell. Edward assumed that Denholm had not been a partner very long. The idea did not bother him. A lawyer in ascendency was better than one on the way down. He wondered what Madeleine would make of him.

Ian Denholm moved and spoke efficiently. He had tea brought in on a tray, and once he'd ascertained that Edward was well enough to answer, posed questions and took notes copiously on an electronic tablet. This interrogation was different from that of the detectives. The questions were searching and precise. Denholm gave him time to think, indeed, he insisted that each response be considered carefully. And he did not ask whether or not his new client had killed Geoffrey Vogel.

Edward volunteered that just to be clear.

"I didn't kill that pompous git."

"Good. That might make it easier to defend you."

"Might?"

Ian Denholm smiled. Madeleine remembered that smile. It invoked a rush of girlish memories. She'd had a massive crush on Ian Denholm at law school. She hadn't seen him since graduation but she'd wondered about him from time to time. Ian's passion had been environmental law back then. It was unlikely he'd be working for a big city criminal law firm, but it was nice to see him nevertheless.

"Bourke says they found Vogel's blood in the sink of my en suite bathroom," Edward said.

"When did they find it?"

"The night I was attacked."

Denholm scowled. "You were attacked in the kitchen, on the ground floor, weren't you? Why were they searching your en suite bathroom?"

"Perhaps they thought someone was still hiding in the bathtub."

Denholm stood, and walked to the window. He looked out. When he turned back, he was smiling again. "Sounds like an illegal search to me."

"And that's good."

"Yes. It could also taint the current warrant."

Edward shook his head. "I still don't understand how—"

"Well, clearly, as you didn't touch Mr. Vogel, it must have come in on someone who did. Possibly it was left in your sink deliberately."

"What do you mean?"

Denholm tapped his stylus against the tablet. "You say that Ms. Meriwether returned with you to your house the evening after Mr. Vogel was killed."

"It was the early hours of the morning by then, but yes."

"And what exactly did you and Ms. Meriwether do?"

"We ate cake and talked."

Denholm waited as if he expected more.

"That's it—we ate cake, drank coffee, and then I took her home."

"Did Ms. Meriwether go upstairs?"

"Yes."

"Forgive me if this is an indelicate question, Mr. McGinnity, but are you and Ms. Meriwether involved?"

"No. We weren't…She went upstairs to get a sweat-shirt."

"Why did she need something to wear?"

"She was cold, I think. Possibly she didn't want to risk spilling cake on her dress."

"So she went into your bedroom alone?" Denholm was clearly sceptical.

"I was making coffee. She knows where everything is. I'm not sure I understand…"

"So Ms. Meriwether might have used your en suite bathroom?"

"Yes. No. You're not suggesting that Vogel's blood came from her?" Edward stood.

"Calm down, Mr. McGinnity. I'm not suggesting anything, just canvassing the possibilities that lead away from the conclusion that the blood was transferred from you."

"Well, that's not a possibility."

Denholm studied him for a moment, and then he went on. "The blood may well have been planted."

"Why would Willow—?"

"By the police or perhaps by the men who assaulted you."

"Again, why—?"

"We are not concerned with why, Mr. McGinnity. It is sufficient that there are other explanations for the presence of Mr. Vogel's blood in your bathroom, since you are adamant that Mr. Vogel himself has never been inside your house."

Edward rubbed his face. The pain at his temples had not yet dissipated completely. "So what do I do now?"

"You go home and clean up."

"Clean up?"

"The police are searching your house, Mr. McGinnity. They're thorough but not often tidy."

Plots

Madeleine stopped, steadied by a familiarity of rhythm. Edward's story was hitting its stride. The plot was gathering a pace and logic and momentum of its own. It would be easier now. One thing would lead to another and she would just have to take it all down. Every book had this moment—when suddenly there was enough, the point of self-perpetuation, when you knew the words would breathe on their own.

She was more than a little intrigued that this story seemed to be inviting so many people from her own memory into its pages. Ian Denholm. She had been so smitten with him at law school. Even now he seemed to glow in recollection. Madeleine laughed. It had been such a silly infatuation. Perhaps Ian had known...he had always been charming and so friendly. Perhaps he pretended not to notice the way she looked at him—a kindness, some form of noblesse oblige, a gracious acceptance of the burden of being so attractive.

This was before she'd met Hugh, of course. The memory was radiant, the perfection of Ian unsullied because she'd never known him particularly well. He'd never had the chance to disappoint her. Thinking of him reminded her of being young and naïve and believing in happily ever after. It was silly, but nice to remember.

Madeleine had fought with Hugh again that morning. She had broached the subject of trying again. He had suggested she see a counsellor to help her come to terms with the last miscarriage and the three before that.

The suggestion had winded her, infuriated her. What the hell was he talking about? She had not sat about weeping, she had not turned to religion making bargains with some god, she had not missed a day of work, she was not some shaking, self-pitying, histrionic wreck. She had only wanted to try again. For that moment, she'd hated Hugh Lamond.

Perhaps this was why Madeleine took such vindictive pleasure in writing Ian Denholm…a kind of secret infidelity. A return to the man she'd loved before Hugh. She cringed. When had she become so ridiculous?

It was the first day of Spring, so clear and bright that the air seemed to sparkle. For the first time in months there was real warmth in the light as it heated the soil and called growing things towards it. Madeleine decided enough was enough. She needed to do something other than write before she became weird. She would weed. In weeks to come, when the tulips showed, she would be glad she had.

She threw on jeans and a cotton jumper, thick socks, and Hugh's work boots. They were a couple of sizes too big but she'd always worn them to garden. She wasn't entirely sure why.

There was still dew in the shadows, those parts of the garden where the sun had not yet placed its drying hand.

It was quiet. Not noiseless, for the house was surrounded by natural bushland which had its own voice—birdsong and the movement of trees—but quiet. Away from the loud silences of the spaces she shared with Hugh. The garden was hers.

Madeleine weeded the little plot beneath the weeping cherry first, pulling the long grass at the base of the cement plinth on which sat her stone cherub. She could feel the sunshine on the back of her neck and shoulders, and the lazy hum of bees about the lavender made it seem somehow warmer. With every miscarriage, Madeleine had planted more bulbs within the box-hedged circle. Perhaps it was some kind of horticultural exorcism; perhaps she'd just need to do something to mark the loss. Green spears, furled and pale, poked from the soil now, and in a short while there would be daffodils and tulips. And perhaps one day there would also be a child.

"Why do you want a child so badly?" Edward stood in the periphery of her vision.

She continued to work the soil. "I don't know. It's just an ache, a kind of panic. I just feel like it's what's next."

"For you?"

"For Hugh and me."

"Hugh doesn't seem so convinced."

Madeleine rocked back onto her heels. Yes. She shrugged. "He'll come round. It's different for men."

"How so?"

"You can't know your child until it's born. Women know their children long before that."

"Because you carry them?"

"Maybe. I don't know. My mother used to say that children are held in their mother's hearts until they are ready to slip down to the womb." She laughed. "Mum had a rather lyrical take on biology. But I guess they do begin in the centre of our bodies. Perhaps that's why they remain in the centre of our thoughts."

Edward glanced at the cement cherub. "Unless they don't stay."

"That's when it's most different...when they don't stay. For men it's just a change in what they expected, what they were preparing for. For women..." She paused trying to find the right words. "Something's changed. There was something there, and there's a space where it once was." Madeleine looked at him, this man in her mind. "You think I'm being melodramatic?"

He shook his head. "No, I'm just wondering why you don't write about this."

"About lost babies?" Her response was fleering. The idea was absurd, ridiculous.

Edward smiled too. Madeleine was aware right then that she liked the way he did so. The expression wasn't dazzling like Ian's, but quiet, as though he did not even realise he was smiling. There was something intimate about it. "Not necessarily," he said, "but why don't you write about the meaning of things, or the lack of meaning? About why you feel, rather than just what you feel."

"Little sadnesses are not a plot, Ned. Everyone has them in some form or another. They aren't a story on their own."

"Perhaps not on their own, but don't you think they are the most interesting part?"

"God, no!"

Edward stepped closer, his eyes fixed on her face as if he were reading each fleeting flicker that crossed her features. "Don't you find people a mystery, Maddie? Isn't every story about why people do what they do?"

She laughed at him, at herself. Why was she having this conversation? Did she doubt the value of her work? When had she become self-conscious?

The breeze caught her hair, blowing a wispy tress across her face. He brushed it back behind her ear with his hand, and again she felt the warmth of his touch. This time she was not startled by the substance of it. Madeleine closed her eyes, not wanting him to dissipate in the bright light of day, or return to the periphery of her vision. She liked him standing close—she could smell his aftershave, sense the rise and fall of his chest as he breathed.

Edward was startled by how physically drawn he was to Madeleine d'Leon then. He'd had conversations with characters before, but this sudden longing was a little odd. Still, he didn't question it. Each story had its own process, its own involvement. The clarity of Madeleine d'Leon, her reality, was exciting. Perhaps it would bring something new to his work. Softly, he touched his lips to hers and when she gasped with surprise it was in the midst of a stolen kiss. He breathed her in, glad he'd not plotted this story in any great detail. It seemed to be choosing paths of its own.

• • ● • •

Edward slammed down the landline.

"What did they say?" Willow was kneeling by the bookshelf, replacing the books that had been pulled out. The search of Edward McGinnity's beach house had been thorough, the rectification less so. The police had taken a few items of clothing, Edward's computers, his mobile phone, and his notebooks. It was the last which Edward was now trying desperately to have returned.

"They're going through them, apparently. Lord knows why my notebooks are of any interest to the police."

Willow's glance was sidelong. "Depends how saucy this new book is. What is your crime-writer getting up to?"

"This isn't funny, Will. How am I supposed to write?"

"Get a new notebook."

Sullenly, Edward rummaged through the kilned-glass basin of Matchbox cars. He retrieved a Morris and ran it across the coffee table. "There are three missing, you know."

"Three what?"

"Three cars."

Willow stared at the basin that must have contained over fifty miniature vehicles. "How could you possibly know that?"

"They're my cars. I know. There's a Mercedes, a Ford, and an Aston Martin missing."

"Perhaps you misplaced them."

"I didn't."

"The men who beat you up—"

"No, the cars were here yesterday."

"So you think the police took your toy cars?"

"Yes."

"Why?"

"They probably didn't think I'd notice."

"Are you saying the police stole your Matchbox cars?"

Edward shrugged. "The cars are gone."

"Perhaps they want to test them—dust them for finger-prints or whatever it is they do these days."

Again, he shrugged.

Willow turned back to the disarrayed books, sorting them into vague categories. Edward's collection of novels had always been eclectic, but it seemed that he had lately been adding a great deal of crime fiction to his shelves.

"Is this research?" she asked, thumbing through a volume by Robotham.

Edward nodded. "I thought I should read a bit of the kind of thing she writes but…" He didn't finish.

"But what?"

"I can't seem to hear her voice in any of these books, I can't get a handle on her as a writer."

"Of course you can't." Willow thumbed through the stack of crime novels. "They're all written by men."

"Is there a difference?"

"Maybe, maybe not, but you might find your Madeleine's literary voice more easily in a female writer. What kind of books does she write?"

"Madeleine? Crime."

"That's only slightly more helpful than saying she writes words. What kind of crime? Does she write thrillers, or police procedurals, or private detectives? Are her books contemporary or historical or—?"

"Historical," Edward said, uncertain why he was sure of this. He hadn't really written about Madeleine's books in such detail. "Early 1900s, I think."

"Perhaps you should read a female historical crimewriter and see if you can hear Madeleine. I think I have a couple. More 1930s than 1900s, but they may help—I'll bring them over."

"I didn't know you read crime fiction."

"I don't read it for the crime."

Edward found himself intrigued. "Then why?"

"For the characters; crime fiction has the sexiest heroes."

"What?"

Willow wrapped her arms around her knees and looked up at him. "The detective is by necessity a delightful combination of intellect, daring, and action." Her gaze was coy. "It's very attractive."

He laughed. "That's a bit like reading *Playboy* for the articles, isn't it?"

"Just the opposite, I would think."

Edward grimaced.

Willow was not having it. "Sweetheart, you know I love your novels. They make me think, they astound me with their artistry, dazzle me with their vocabulary, and when I've finished reading I'm mentally exhausted and probably cleverer than I once was. But you know, sometimes I read books because I want to fall in love." She shrugged. "Call me shallow."

"You fall in love with fictional detectives?"

"Invariably. Something very hot about a man following a lead."

"I'll make a note."

"So," she said, her eyes sparkling, "what do you plan to do about your missing toys?"

"Must you call them toys? They're very valuable collectibles."

"Oh. How much are they worth?"

"About ten cents each." He frowned. "I think I'll forget that they were here yesterday, notice that they've vanished and go see Bourke."

"I don't follow."

"I'll tell him I think the men who broke in here must have taken them."

"Nope...still don't follow."

"Well, they'll either have to include the theft of the cars in the investigation as some kind of lead, or admit they took them."

"You're not serious."

"I am. It's bad enough that three thugs break in here and beat the hell out of me, without then being robbed by the flaming police."

Willow shoved the last of the books into the shelf. "They're old Matchbox cars, Ned."

Madeleine tapped the arm of her writing chair, her face set with contemplation. She wondered what she was doing with the cars. Were they simply some kind of motif, or would they play a crucial part in the plot? Was there something behind Edward's reaction? His anger that someone would take his toys was endearingly childlike, but she did wonder why.

"They were Jacob's. Well, Jacob's and mine." Edward looked directly at Madeleine. "We were always fighting about who owned which car."

"Your brother?" Willow asked gently. "Ned, look at me—I didn't know. I'm sorry—of course you must get them back." She patted the carpet beside her for him to sit and waited till he did so.

"I have chairs, you know," he grumbled, as he lowered himself gingerly to the floor.

Willow bit her lower lip and winced. "Oh bugger, I forgot. How are you feeling?"

"Still a bit sore, but I'm fine."

"Were you close?" Willow asked. "Your brother and you?"

"Sometimes...sometimes we couldn't bear each other." Edward smiled as he remembered. His eyes were focussed distantly. Once again it seemed to Madeleine that he was speaking directly to her. "Jake liked the vintage models best. My mother declared all the cars jointly owned to stop us fighting, but we always knew who owned what."

"I'm sure he'd be happy that you still have them." Willow rubbed his arm.

"I think he'd be a bit put out that I took them all out of their boxes," Edward confessed. "Jake was a bit precious about that sort of thing."

"He didn't play with them?"

"Oh, yes, we'd play with them, but he'd always return them to their boxes. He was naturally tidy. Might have ended up an accountant if..." He stopped. It was hardest to consider what his siblings might have been, what they might have done together. His sister had been just a baby, but he and Jacob had had plans, childish, competitive declarations of what they would become. "Jake was going to be a judge."

"A judge? Of what?" Willow asked. It seemed an odd ambition for a little boy.

"A legal send-you-to-gaol-type judge. I'd wanted to be a policeman back then, you see. Jake was two years younger—he was trying to one-up me, I guess. We thought that judges were in charge of the police back then." He shook his head. "I was furious. But I'd already declared I was going to be a policeman. There was some kind of nine-year-old code that said I couldn't change my mind, so I was stuck. Couldn't think of who'd be in charge of a judge, anyway…"

"It's all very law and order." Willow leaned against him. "I wanted to be a cat burglar." She cupped her hands on either side of her head. "I somehow thought I'd have the ears."

Edward chuckled. He'd never met Willow's parents. Perhaps she was from a family of career criminals. It'd make sense in some ways. It was an interesting story idea…perhaps when he'd finished with Madeleine.

Madeleine frowned as she wrote the thought. Of course there would be other stories, but not yet…not even soon.

Willow took a deep breath. "I think I should sack Andy."

"What? Why?"

"So he can be your lawyer. He's going to be furious when he hears what happened."

Edward's nose wrinkled. "I have a lawyer."

"Yes, but Andy's more than just a lawyer."

Edward shrugged. "You need him more than I do. I'll speak to Andy."

Negotiations

The Writers' Bar, which served as a green room at the Final Word Writers' Festival, was quiet at eight in the morning. It seemed writers were not early risers. Located within a refurbished wharf building, the bar was large and dimly lit. A central kitchen offered every species of coffee to the few early birds seated in the studded leather booths.

Madeleine d'Leon was having breakfast with Leith Henry before appearing on a panel called "Once Were Lawyers." As the title suggested her fellow panellists had also come from the legal profession.

"I'm sorry, Maddie. They don't like it." Leith placed her hands flat on the table as she delivered the reaction to the three chapters Madeleine had submitted. "They think you risk alienating your readership."

"My readership? Why?"

"They've invested a lot of money building your profile as a certain type of writer. They don't think this new novel fits."

"Why not?"

"They say the novel doesn't know what it is: crime fiction, memoir, literary fiction…"

"Novels have to have a sense of identity now?" Madeleine snapped.

"Apparently this one is too much of a hybrid. They believe the voice is confused."

"It is not!" Madeleine could hear how childish she sounded. Worse, she could feel herself tearing up.

Leith paused. "Tarquin feels that Edward McGinnity is too introspective for a crime hero, and not active enough."

"Active? Do they want him to swing from chandeliers?"

Leith smiled. "Possibly, especially if he was shooting a gun at the same time. They don't think the public will like him. They'd like to see another Veronica Killwilly book as soon as possible." She paused. "They have a serious offer for the television rights for the Killwilly series."

"From whom?"

"Grand Oak Productions. They'd like you to write the first screenplay."

Madeleine shook her head. "I can't right now."

"It's an excellent offer, Maddie."

"Does it hinge on me writing the screenplay?"

"Maybe."

"Could you ask? And could you ask again about Ned?"

Leith sighed. "It's not personal, Maddie. It's all about marketing. They're concerned that promoting you as anything but an easy-to-read crime-writer will dilute sales and impact all your books."

"What do you think?" Madeleine braced herself.

"There are other publishers, but it's a little risky. Tarquin may decide to stop publishing you altogether, especially if they lose this deal with Grand Oak Productions."

For a moment Madeleine said nothing, stunned, hurt. She blinked, scrabbling for dignity. "I meant what do you think about what I'm writing?"

"Honestly?"

"Of course."

"I agree that this new novel doesn't fit neatly anywhere, but that's life. Very few things fit neatly. I still think it could be your best work. That said, Maddie, it's not always just about writing a good book."

"I can't stop writing this, Leith."

"Good. I want to see how it comes out."

"What about—?"

"Publication? Leave that to me. As long as you're ready to leave Tarquin Press and lose the television deal? You've been with them from the beginning and if things go badly you could be betting the Veronica Killwilly series on this new book."

Madeleine hesitated. She had never seriously contemplated being published by anyone other than Tarquin Press. "You really think they'd stop publishing Veronica?"

"They might, and since they own your backlist, it'd be difficult to take it to a new publisher. Veronica's sales are respectable and quite lucrative, and you review well, but I'm afraid you're not big enough yet to call the shots, Maddie."

"What do you think I should do?"

Leith cut into her poached eggs. "Do you think you can start writing another Killwilly novel now?"

"But I haven't finished—"

"Could you work on both?"

Madeleine groaned. "Yes, I suppose I could."

"Good. Do that. Let's keep everybody happy. Tarquin just needs to know that they'll get their Killwilly in time for a Christmas release. And that you might, in time, be willing to write the screenplay."

"Are you sure you can't talk them round to—"

Leith added salt. "Yes, I'm sure. Maddie, I know you like the people at Tarquin, but they're not the right fit for your new novel."

Madeleine sighed. "I know. I just feel disloyal."

Leith sat back, shaking her head as she did so. "They have other writers, Maddie. Publishing is not a monogamous business. It's time to start believing in what you're writing and playing the field."

Madeleine smiled. "Take it from me, believing in what I'm writing is not the problem." She stared at the smashed avocado on sourdough before her. She could feel Edward watching her even now. Waiting for her next move.

Leith was right. The relationship with Tarquin was a business partnership, not a creative one. But Madeleine felt wounded and slightly humiliated all the same. "Okay, do whatever you need to."

Madeleine stared at the signing table in dismay. They'd seated her next to Tom Keneally, for pity's sake. There were already five hundred odd people waiting in line for him. She sighed. It wouldn't be art without the ritual humiliation.

Angela Savage hooked an arm through hers. She, too, had a place at the signing table, but it wasn't so close to the festival's star.

"Oh, bugger," Angela's voice was sympathetic. "At least you'll get a photo with Keneally," she offered in consolation.

Madeleine grimaced. "Unlikely to get a clear shot through this crowd."

"There're few people with your books." Angela said, as they manoeuvred through Keneally's hordes to take their seats at the signing table. Madeleine welcomed the elderly gentleman who stepped forward to have her autograph her latest novel. It was a genuine greeting, grateful, if a little eager. She did not hurry their conversation and composed a lengthy inscription for his book. In this way, the half dozen persons in her line would last at least thirty minutes. Fortunately, none of them seemed in any urgent haste.

Madeleine could see Edward laughing. She ignored him and signed and chatted and then sat clicking her pen as Keneally's readers tried to avoid eye contact. She wondered idly if Edward McGinnity accepted festival invitations. Somehow, she thought not. But why?

"Because the work isn't about me," he said.

"No...but you're behind it."

He looked away from her for a moment. His hands were plunged deep into his pockets. "I appeared at one of those in-conversation interviews just after my book was shortlisted. They wanted to talk about the accident. Apparently, that was my story."

Madeleine understood then. Writers were required to have a story aside from that which they wrote, to become a character spun off from their own books. Tragedy was a publicist's gold, and if they found a vein, they'd mine it relentlessly. Not to be cruel, but because it was their job to make a writer memorable, and nothing lingered in the recollection like suffering. Unless it was humour, she supposed, thinking of Tom Keneally. Readers wanted you to either make them laugh or cry, in your books or in person. It was not surprising. To the reader, the author was an extension of his or her work and not the other way around.

"What happened to your family is part of your work, you know," she told him gently. "It's written into all your books."

"You've read my books?" he asked.

"Of course I have, I'm writing you."

He gazed at her and, though he still smiled, she could see pain in the unblinking wideness of his eyes.

"There's a deep sadness at the heart of your work," she said. "People are drawn to it."

"Why would they be drawn to sadness?"

"It's the irony of compassion, I suppose."

"The deaths of my family are not entertainment, Maddie."

"They're not looking to be entertained, they're hoping to understand."

"You have a great deal of faith in my readers."

"When they read your book, they put a great deal of faith in you. It seems fair."

Edward recalled a conversation with his agent. Leith had said something similar about the trust readers place in the writer, though he couldn't remember her exact words. Regardless, it seemed he was placing a version of it on the lips of Madeleine d'Leon. "So you come to festivals out of some sense of obligation?"

"No, I come because they're fun. Because I like talking to other writers." She studied him. "Don't you?"

"I talk to you, don't I?"

"Say bestseller!" Angela snapped a photo, holding the phone at an angle that would make it hard to distinguish Tom Keneally's signing line from Madeleine d'Leon's.

Madeleine cringed as she watched her friend post the picture online. "I suspect that's fraud."

Angela shrugged. "You're a lawyer…you'll get me off."

With nothing left to sign and some hours before either was to appear again, they left the table to find lunch. In this, Madeleine deferred to her colleague. Angela Savage's protagonist was a crime-solving food critic. Consequently Angela had eaten at most of the city's restaurants in the interests of research.

"So what are you working on?" Madeleine asked as they sat down at Bahn Thai, apparently famous for its dumplings. The restaurant's décor was functional, the chairs, tablecloths, and flowers all plastic. But every seat was taken, and a good proportion of the clientele were of Asian extraction. It was a noisy, aromatic place where taste and company were all that mattered.

"I'm writing a children's book." Angela ordered for them both mid-conversation. "A picture book for the children of foodies… *We're Going on a Truffle Hunt.*"

"Are you serious?" Madeleine was already laughing.

Angela's response was wickedly gleeful. "Oh, yes. The ultimate quest epic for the first-world child. Purple Duck is getting Tony Flowers."

"Really?" Madeleine's eyes widened. Tony Flowers was one of the most sought-after book illustrators in the country. His involvement all but guaranteed the project's success.

Angela nodded happily. "I might finally have a book that sells out its advance. Children's books are the only things that seem to be moving at the moment."

Madeleine had heard that said before. When money was tight, people cut back on their own reading indulgences long before they were willing to deny their children books. Perhaps it was instinctive parental sacrifice or a fear that any deprivation would be irreversibly detrimental. As a result, the stringent economic times were being felt primarily by writers of adult books. Advances were plummeting and even established authors were being dropped by their publishers.

They talked of Angela's picture book as they ate dumplings and drank peach iced tea. And then they moved to a French bakery for cake and coffee and to exchange gossip about the industry.

"So I hear on the grapevine that you're looking for a new publisher."

Madeleine choked on her cappuccino. "No...well, maybe...I mean how did you—?"

"Settle, petal, it's not common knowledge. I just happened to see your agent coming out of Harry Lewin's office."

"Harry Lewin?"

"He's the commissioning editor at Purple Duck."

"I'm not Leith's only client," Madeleine said, thinking of Edward McGinnity. She shook her head at the absurdity of that train of thought.

"I had a meeting with Harry later that day. He asked about you."

"What did he want to know?"

"Just background stuff…your backlist, what you're like to work with, that sort of thing."

"Oh."

"So, am I right? Are you shopping?"

"Tarquin doesn't want my latest manuscript. Leith is checking my options."

"Why don't they like it?"

"Something about my market. They want to me to shut up and write Veronica Killwilly until the cows come home."

Angela sighed. "It's easier to show a one-trick pony. Still, you must really believe in this new manuscript if you're willing to risk everything. Tarquin Press is a good operation."

"Yes, I think I am beginning to believe in it. Perhaps too much."

"Too much?"

Madeleine winced, retracting the confession. "I didn't mean that. I'm just living and breathing the manuscript at the moment. Sometimes I have to remind myself what's real."

Angela sighed. "Are your literary constructs taking over? Therein lies madness, my friend." She formed her fingers into a gun. "Kill them off quickly before they enslave you!"

"I'm not sure I can without taking myself out as well." Madeleine propped her elbows on the table. "Veronica Killwilly always seemed to have an existence independent of me too, but not like Edward. Sometimes it feels like he's making the decisions."

"Decisions about what?"

"About what happens next."

Angela smiled, sympathetically, or perhaps knowingly. Madeleine wasn't sure. She asked.

"Does this happen to you, Ang?"

Angela shrugged. "I think it happens to every writer to some degree. Who knows what's really going on in our poor beleaguered, broken-down intoxicated brains? I'm not sure it's a good idea to look too closely into the mechanics of what we do; it may break the spell."

Madeleine nodded. "It's just that sometimes I feel like I'm on the precipice of going too far."

"In fiction? No such thing, my friend." Angela sipped her coffee, pausing to lick white froth from the scarlet bow of her upper lip. "If you're nervous, it's because you're pushing yourself further than in your previous novels. It'll strengthen the work."

Madeleine said nothing. She hadn't really been thinking about the quality of her writing. Angela interpreted the silence as a concern about just that.

"I wouldn't worry about it, Maddie." She cut each of the two desserts they'd ordered in half. "It's a book. Actually, it's not even a book…it's a potential book. Nobody's going to live or die. Just write, see what happens. You can always rewrite it if it doesn't work."

Madeleine bit her lip as she weighed the advice. Angela was right, but Madeleine recoiled from the idea that a story be changed once told. The process seemed unnatural somehow. Of course she polished prose, replaced words and restructured sentences, just like any other writer, but she didn't ever alter what happened. To Madeleine d'Leon, the act of placing words on a page cast her imagined events into a kind of actuality which she could no more change than she could history. She left that to better writers, disciplined wordsmiths who could bring themselves to undo what they'd done.

Even so, there was comfort in Angela's counsel, a collegiate empathy—a knowledge of what it was to scrabble for words that would make sense of the world both within and without. Fleeting, slippery inspiration that defied any sort of restraint.

In the corner of her eye, Madeleine saw Edward McGinnity smile. He knew already that she would change nothing.

A Pursuit of Justice

The gallery was in the process of bumping out the Willow Meriwether exhibition before hanging the next. Paintings were being taken down for packing and shipping to the art lovers and dealers who'd acquired them. The process was one of organised activity, bubble wrap, and paperwork.

Willow was watching as her grand debut was dismantled when Edward came in. A concerned curator intercepted him and asked his business.

"Ned! Hello!" Willow intervened and introduced Edward McGinnity. "Ned is my very dear friend. He's come to support me…it is so very emotional watching one's work come down."

The curator smiled, mauve lips, bright even teeth. "You should be delighted! I don't know of many people who sell out their first exhibition." She whispered, her hand splayed beside her mouth. "I believe your agent is being inundated with offers to host your next show."

Willow managed to blush. "Yes, Adrian would be furious if he knew I was here and not at home painting. Still…" She gazed beseechingly at the curator. "Someone should be here to see the exhibition off."

Eventually, the curator was persuaded that the show needed some sort of farewell. She handed Edward a security pass and waved them in.

They wandered amongst the activity, Willow telling Edward who had purchased each of her paintings: several private collectors and a corporate entity. Chearles Pty Ltd had acquired the majority of the works for what Edward presumed a tax-deductible display in a boardroom or foyer. Soon they became unnoticed, as the curators worked to restore the gallery to pristine emptiness. As soon as Edward sensed that they were no longer of any interest, he guided Willow towards the fire stairs in which Vogel had died. The police cordon had been removed and the landing cleaned.

"What are you doing?" Willow asked.

"I just wanted to have another look."

"Why?"

"I'm trying to get it clear in my head how Vogel might have been lured into the fire stairs and murdered without anyone noticing." Edward scanned the stairwell. "You know, it's almost ironic that they don't put fire alarms in the fire escape."

Willow looked up at the ceiling several floors above. "You're right, there's no alarm."

"Vogel was a smoker, wasn't he?"

Willow nodded. "Yes. He used one of those Bakelite cigarette holders. Do you think he came in here to smoke?"

Edward started down the stairs. "He might have joined his killer here for a covert cigarette."

"That might explain why no one noticed him being forced into the escape—he snuck out voluntarily."

"So the killer could be someone he knows."

"Who smokes," Willow added.

"Could be." Edward ran his eyes over the recently scrubbed landing on which they'd seen the body, not really sure what he was looking for. "Do you have a guest list for the opening, Will?"

"I could get one."

"Would you please?"

"Of course. But why?"

"It's a place to start. I presume there'll be names we can eliminate straight away and we'll look through the others for those who Vogel might have joined for a cigarette."

"So you're…investigating?"

"Just looking into it."

"The police—"

"Are idiots…not to mention they think I did it, so they're unlikely to listen to my theories."

"You have a theory?"

"Nothing more than that the killer smokes…maybe."

Willow's smile curled gently to the right. "And you can't think of any other reason someone, or two, may wish to slip out of a crowded party into the privacy of a fire escape?"

"Vogel? You can't be serious."

"There's somebody for everybody, Ned."

"So I'm told." He shrugged. "We'll check the guest list for any potential mystery seductresses as well…How many blind, deaf, and dumb women could possibly be attending an art exhibition?"

"You'd be surprised," Willow murmured.

Edward ran up the stairs and held open the door back into the exhibition rooms. "After you."

They slipped back in. It seemed no one had noticed their retreat into the fire escape, or perhaps the watching world had simply assumed it a tryst. The artist was, after all, married and the young man was clearly besotted.

Edward's eyes were directed above once again. "There're security cameras on every painting, Will. One of them must have caught something."

"Surely the police will have thought of that?"

"Yes, you're right. Still, I wouldn't mind seeing that footage."

Willow folded her arms. "I might be able to help you with that, if you think it's important."

"You? How? The police aren't going to release the footage to either of us."

Willow laughed. "You really are a Luddite sometimes, Ned! We're not talking about videotapes…the security system is digital. It would take seconds to download another copy of the footage."

"And you can do this?" Edward was sceptical.

"I know one of the guys who works in security. We'll buy a memory card at the gift shop and drop by and see him before we leave, if you like."

Madeleine watched the exchange carefully. There was something casually devious about Willow Meriwether—she slipped so easily into espionage. The writer found herself wondering about the artist.

Edward and Willow remained in the exhibition hall for only a few more minutes while Willow called her acquaintance in security. "Lou's made the appropriate access changes to our security passes," she said as she returned the mobile phone to her pocket. "We can just go down."

Security was based on the ground floor in a control room which contained video feeds from every part of the gallery. When the writer and the artist came in, Lou Mattlock was nowhere to be seen. Then Willow noticed the grunting and followed the sound behind the console where they discovered a young guard doing sit-ups. He held up his hand for them to wait until he completed his set, finishing with an explosive count of "hundred." He grabbed the towel hanging over the office chair and wiped his neck as he stood to speak with them. "Gotta drop a few pounds, you know," he said apologetically. He patted his belly. "I'm on the desk this entire month."

"You definitely look thinner," Willow said. "They're bound to accept you soon, Lou!"

The guard beamed and Willow introduced him to Edward McGinnity. "We have a favour to ask you, Lou."

"Sure thing. Whaddaya need?"

"We were hoping to see the footage you gave the police. Of my opening."

Mattlock's eyes narrowed. "Why?"

Willow appeared to hesitate. She glanced at the door and lowered her voice. "There's a man. He's been bothering me for months—turning up at my studio, sending flowers, following me. I think he might have been there that night."

"Have you told the police?" Mattlock straightened his shoulders.

Willow shook her head emphatically. "I'm not sure he was there, you see, and I don't want to give the police his name unless I'm sure. He's an important man, very powerful in the art world. I don't want to invite trouble if I don't have to."

Edward said nothing. Clearly Willow had this in hand.

"You did keep a copy of the footage you gave the police, didn't you?"

The security guard wavered. "Yes, it's on the backup hard disk, but I don't think I'm strictly supposed to."

"Please, Lou. I don't want to overreact, but I'm frightened." She held out the USB stick they bought at the gallery shop.

He sighed and took it. "You'll delete it once you're finished, right?"

"Of course…and if anything goes wrong, I'll say I hacked the gallery system to get the footage. Ned will say he saw me do it, won't you Ned?"

"Indeed, I saw you hack…helped even."

Mattlock walked around the console. About forty screens had been displaying surveillance of the gallery while he did sit-ups. He inserted the USB stick into a port, typed for a while, and pressed Return with flourish.

"Thank you, Lou. You're a true friend."

"If you'd like me to speak to this bloke who's following you," the guard said, puffing up. "A quiet word from a law man might be all it takes."

Willow smiled sweetly. "I'll keep that in mind."

"I'd be happy to help, that's all," Mattlock handed her the memory stick.

Edward felt a twinge of compassion, perhaps camaraderie, for the guard. "Would you like to join us for lunch, Lou?" he asked. "It's the least we could do."

"No thanks, mate. I still have a stone or so to lose before they accept me."

And so they took their leave of the security guard.

"Is he trying to get into the police force?" Edward asked as they walked out to his car.

"Lou? No, not at all."

"Then what's he trying to lose weight for?"

"He wants to donate his body to science. Apparently they only take skinny bodies…something about it being hard to store human fat. It's odd. I would have thought every body was of some use or interest to science."

"That's not the part that's odd."

"You mean Lou?" She laughed. "Poor man has a very domineering mother. He still lives at home. I think this is his way of ensuring that he'll escape her clutches eventually."

"By donating his body?"

"A final act of rebellion when he is beyond the consequences. He's quite dedicated to the idea."

Madeleine giggled as she contemplated weaving Lou Mattlock further into the story somehow. She liked the idea of him. She made a note to herself to check the veracity of the claim that Science was interested only in lean cadavers. She had heard it before in passing but couldn't remember whether the information came from a reliable source. A little part of her was tempted to follow Lou Mattlock for a while, but she felt the tug of the surveillance footage and returned her watch to Edward and Willow.

"We have to stop by the shops." Edward started the Jaguar.

"What shops? Why?"

"The police took all my computers. I'll have to buy a new laptop if we're going to watch this."

"Buy a new laptop?" Willow rolled her eyes. "Have you never heard of a library? We can use one of their computers."

"There'll be a few hours of footage, Will. And, unless libraries have changed significantly, they don't give you a private room and a pot of coffee with your computer... both of which we'll need."

"But a new computer, just for—"

"I'm a writer. I need a computer and I have no idea how long the police will hold onto my old one."

Willow sighed but she said nothing further. It was probably ridiculous to argue about extravagance when they were both under the threat of arrest for murder.

Indifferent to price, Edward made his purchase quickly and they drank ice cream spiders in the department store café while waiting for the appropriate software to be loaded.

"This is all rather exciting." Willow fidgeted with the USB stick. "Your crime-writer would approve, I think."

"Approve of what? Don't lose that."

Willow put the USB back into her pocket. "Of your investigating. It's classic crime fiction—the innocent bystander finds his back against the wall and is forced to take action, accepting the mantle of hero in the pursuit of justice."

Madeleine winced. But there was no point pretending she was reinventing crime fiction, as so many writers and their publicists appeared fond of claiming.

Edward was a little perturbed to hear himself described as a cliché. But it didn't seem as though he had any choice but to be just that. "Madeleine would probably have solved this by now," he said absently.

"Rubbish," Madeleine objected. "I have no idea who did it yet. You'll just have to investigate, even if it is beneath you."

He smiled at her. "It's not beneath me. I'd just rather be writing."

"Ned!" Willow caught his attention again. "You were a thousand miles away."

"Sorry." He checked his watch. "Come on, let's pick up the computer and solve this mystery. You do understand that the hero has to get the girl in the end, don't you?"

Willow squinted at him. "You could just keep the one in your head."

They returned to Edward's beach house to watch the footage. Edward waved at the unmarked police car that had been following them before stepping inside. "I wonder if I should send them out a drink?"

"They're on duty."

"Coffee?"

"I'm sure your lawyer would tell you not to goad the police."

He pulled a tin of ground coffee from the refrigerator. "Just us, then."

Willow moved the kilned bowl of Matchbox cars and set the new laptop on the coffee table. They sat together on the couch and watched. The footage was taken from a number of cameras within the gallery space. They scrolled through to find the footage from the camera trained on *Literatum scripius excellio*. It didn't cover the fire stairs specifically but anybody who went to the fire door, or the men's room would have to pass before it.

It picked up the conversation between Vogel, Willow, and Edward. Edward's disdain, his loathing of Vogel was clearly visible on the footage. It showed Edward's departure and a little later both Willow and Vogel joining other conversations.

Edward checked the time on the tape. "Right, we know he was alive to this point. We're interested in who passes in front of the camera from left to right from now onwards."

Willow frowned. "Explain that to me."

"The fire stairs are on the left of the screen. The killer would have been coming from there."

"Assuming he returned to the opening. He might have simply walked down the stairs and out of the building via another floor."

Edward groaned. "Dammit. You're right. This is no use whatsoever."

Madeleine paused, disappointed, frustrated. She'd hoped this thread would lead to something. The practicalities had not been something she'd anticipated. Perhaps, if the camera was trained directly on the door to the fire stairs? No. That would be too ridiculously convenient and solve the mystery entirely too easily, not to mention too soon. She groaned, cursing internally as she considered cutting the sequence. If the footage wasn't going to progress the plot somehow, then it didn't belong in the story. But now that it was written it became what happened and she resisted going back.

"Hold on," Willow said as Edward stood. "Let's just watch it. We may see something anyway—someone who wasn't on the guest list or someone who left before the body was discovered."

Edward stopped. He sat back down and grimaced at the artist. "You can see why I don't write crime fiction."

"I can, rather," she replied, settling into the couch and putting her feet on the coffee table. "Now shut up and watch or go make popcorn."

Madeleine listened to the gentle rise and fall of Hugh snoring beside her as she stared at the ceiling. They'd just made love for the first time in weeks. It was strange…a mechanical angry act. When Hugh finally came, the relief was more to do with the fact that it was over than any physical ecstasy. He'd touched her body like he was tuning a television, pressing buttons with an expectation that results would follow, irritated when they didn't. She'd been tense, and handling what might once have aroused her was uncomfortable and intrusive. She'd wanted to push him away and she suspected that he had wished she would. But she hadn't and neither had he and now they could not take it back, could not stop the creeping chill between them.

Madeleine turned her back to Hugh's form, curling around the privacy of her own thoughts. She wasn't sure why he'd suddenly wanted her. She'd not made an excuse because she'd hoped it might help her sleep. It seemed ridiculous now, weak. She'd agreed to sex seeking sleep, because she hoped post-coital languor would grant her unconsciousness. Perhaps Hugh had, too…for him, success.

But the kiss, Edward McGinnity's stolen kiss. It played on her mind now, in the darkness when she lay alone beside her husband. She remembered a time when she and Hugh were first in love, when they had kissed endlessly. Intensely. Excitedly. Their hearts pressed against each other's. When they'd first become intimate, it would have been impossible to separate the kissing out, but slowly that had changed. Over the years it had retreated. Now they had managed to make love without bringing their lips anywhere near the other's body. It had been all hands and organs, no breath, no words, a joining without connection. They'd fucked at a distance. How had it come to this?

But there was Edward's kiss, too easily brought to mind because that's where it had always been. Gentle, lingering. She held the feeling of it now and closed herself around it, cradling it, desperate to fall asleep within it. But sleep would not come. Instead she thought about the security footage Edward and Willow had procured, watched it over again, searching, looking. There had to be something. Some little thing, a clue, a red herring, a reason...

"Maybe there's nothing," Edward whispered. "Maybe it's a path you went down just so you could know there was nothing there."

"I don't want to delete it."

"Why would you delete it? It was what happened. It failed, but that doesn't mean it shouldn't have ever happened."

Madeleine could feel the pillow wet under her cheek.

"Everything has to progress the story," she said.

"Why?" He pushed a stray tress of hair behind her ear, tracing the curve of her cheek with his fingertips. "Not everything is about moving forward. Sometimes it's about taking a step back. Trying something else."

Madeleine watched Edward's lips as he spoke. But she closed her eyes when those lips pressed against hers, softly parting until she could taste him, feel him tasting her. Edward's hand moved down from her face, light upon her neck, until it cupped her breast. She froze, afraid any movement now would wake Hugh, but she did not resist. Edward's mouth followed the path his hand had taken. His tongue swirled against her skin and his hand slid lower still. "Ned," she whispered.

His lips were on hers again then and her back arched towards him. Gradually, he brought up his knee, parting her legs to allow him access, his fingers first, gentle, exploring, as he sucked the skin on her throat. Madeleine's breath became ragged. He languished there, unhurried, smiling as he saw the almost bewildered desire in her face. He waited until she was shuddering before he entered and found welcome. Slowly, inch by inch, he claimed a place in her body.

Madeleine felt pleasure explode and spread into every quivering nerve. It seemed a star had burst within her, casting constellations into all the unlit parts of herself, as she lay trembling beneath him. She kissed her lover's chest, tasting the slight salt of his skin, sensing the beat of his heart against her lips. His hands pressed into the small of her back as he took her more urgently now. She moved with him, went with him.

When Edward's body finally tensed, claimed by release and descent from that carnal peak, he did not look away or retreat to some solitary place, but stayed with her, his gaze locked on hers, so that she could see the reflection of her own surprised desire in his eyes. He kissed her as they floated down, spent, tangled, together.

Evidence

Breakfast was strange.

Hugh had always preferred to treat sex as if it had never happened from the moment it was done. He was amorous enough in the lead-up, but the moment the whole business was complete, he seemed to dust off his hands and sleep, or want to talk of politics or work. It was as if the act of sex embarrassed him somehow. Madeleine had once found this post-coital routine quaint and now she was at least accustomed to it.

This morning, however, Hugh patted her behind when he reached around her to grab the kettle.

She looked at him surprised. He averted his eyes. "Do you want a coffee?"

"Yes," she said after a moment.

And so they ate together, an odd, polite meal that left Madeleine a little bewildered. They talked about the new Marvel movie. "We should try to see it," Hugh said.

"Yes…I'd like that."

"Maybe one day we'll be able to go to the premiere of the Veronica Killwilly movie."

Madeleine tensed. She hadn't mentioned the Grand Oak Productions offer…how could Hugh know?

"You'll have to wear something other than pyjamas." Hugh raised his eyes and looked at her for the first time. He pulled back. "What's that on your neck?"

"Where?" Madeleine was immediately self-conscious.

Hugh reached over the table and pulled back the collar of her pyjama top. "My God, they're love bites."

Madeleine got up and checked her reflection in the sideboard mirror. There were a series of bruises on her throat, small but distinct.

"Did I do that?" Hugh asked puzzled. Neither of them could remember him kissing her neck.

"No…It was the sailors I keep under the bed for emergencies." She pulled her collar back to hide at least some of the telltale bruises.

Hugh frowned, too perplexed by the appearance of the marks to even pretend to be amused. "I'd best get off to work. I'll be late again tonight."

As soon as he had left, Madeleine returned to the mirror. They were unmistakeable. Small swirling smudges, purple against the mortified flush of her skin. She stared in horror, though, even now, her skin tingled and her heart hastened with the memory of Edward's tongue against her throat.

But how could a dream, however intense, leave bruises in its wake? Madeleine gazed at her own reflection, struggling to suppress her rising guilt. She had fantasised about another man whilst her husband slept beside her…surely that was adultery on some level.

She fingered the chunky bracelet on her right wrist. Had she forgotten to take it off the night before? Had she slept with her hand wedged beneath her neck? Yes, that must have been it. What else could it have been?

The possibility afforded her relief, though she wasn't sure what against. Perhaps it was that she was only guilty of an imaginary infidelity.

Unsettled, Madeleine retreated to the certain morality of her imagined world.

The screen displayed her last paragraph with the inevitable blankness beneath. Edward and Willow sat forward on the couch, elbows on knees, eyes fixed on the laptop between them.

And then they saw it, both at once. Edward sat back and looked at her, waiting, allowing Willow to react first. She moved forward, her head tilted, her eyes large. "Fuck," she whispered. "That's Elliot."

Edward nodded. "It is."

Willow stood. "I have to go home."

"I'm coming with you."

She didn't argue.

• • ● • •

Elliot Kaufman opened the door with a fried turkey drumstick in his other hand and grease on his lips. "Willy—there you are, baby. Fuck off, McGinnity!"

Edward ignored him, stepping in behind Willow and closing the door behind them.

"What the hell were you doing at my launch?" Willow hurled straight in.

"I wasn't—"

"Liar! We saw you on the security footage!" Willow pushed Kaufman furiously.

He stood firm. "You're spying on me now?"

Edward intervened. "Look, Kaufman, if we saw you, you can bet the police have or will too."

"This is nothing to do with you, McGinnity!"

"What were you doing at the gallery, Elliot?" Willow demanded. She was on the verge of tears, a fact which heated Edward's blood and cooled Elliot's.

"I was supporting my wife." His lips twitched upwards.

"You said you weren't coming!" Willow snapped.

"Yeah, I did, but I knew it was important to you," Kaufman said quietly.

"Why didn't you...?"

"When I got there, I saw you hanging off this fuckwit!" He cast his glare towards Edward. "Figured I wasn't wanted!"

Willow's face softened. "Oh, Elliot."

"Every time you step out with him, baby," his voice cracked, "I wonder if you'll ever come back to me."

Edward rolled his eyes, but Willow reached up to stroke the carefully groomed stubble on Kaufman's cheek. "Elliot...I'm sorry...I didn't think—"

Kaufman leaned down and kissed her...deep, lingering, territorial. Edward shook his head.

"You can fuck off now, McGinnity," Kaufman snarled as he pulled Willow into his chest, the turkey drumstick still in his hand.

"Why haven't you said anything before about being at the gallery?" Edward persisted.

"Nobody asked."

"When did you leave?"

"How many times do I have to tell you to fuck off?"

"Ned," Willow cautioned as Edward flared.

"Will, you're not buying his—?"

"That's enough, Ned! Perhaps you should go. I'll see you soon."

Edward looked at her, silently pleading for her to see sense.

"Ned...please."

Kaufman smiled.

Edward ignored him and focussed on Willow.

And in her eyes he saw that she truly wished he'd go.

• • ● • •

Ian Denholm tapped notes into his tablet. "I'll run a background check on Elliot Kaufman," he said without looking up. "What do you know about him?"

Edward rubbed his brow, aware that Willow would hate him for what he was doing. "He's an artist...works in oils and collage."

"Successful?"

"I don't think so. Willow's the talent."

"What else?"

"He's a bastard."

"That's not necessarily a crime. Would he kill Vogel to protect his wife's reputation?"

Edward shrugged. He had always thought Kaufman jealous of Willow's success. It seemed to him more likely that he would have relished the dimming of her star.

"How does Kaufman feel about you?" Denholm prompted.

"The loathing is mutual."

"Clearly, he's not a possessive man."

"What makes you say that?"

"Well, he appears to tolerate the time you and Ms. Meriwether spend together."

"That has more to do with confidence than anything

else," Edward replied sullenly. "Kaufman is certain of Willow's affections."

"Is he wrong to be?"

Edward sighed. "No. She loves him. Would do anything for him. If he asked her to never see me again, she would probably agree."

"No she wouldn't!" Madeleine protested. "She's not like that. She has a backbone!"

"This is not the first exhibition Willow's been offered," Edward replied, looking past Denholm at her. "She's passed on bigger opportunities…asked them to offer the show to Kaufman instead. She's constantly dodging and weaving so he doesn't fall into her shadow. He knows it. He allows it."

"You're underestimating her," Madeleine said, unsure of why she felt so strongly. "Women sacrifice their dreams for love all the time. That doesn't mean she'd do that to you!"

His brow arched and he seemed about to respond when Denholm asked, "Why do you think he hasn't demanded she never see you?"

"As I said, he's confident."

Denholm frowned. "I'd be surprised if that was all there was to it. Has Ms. Meriwether ever asked you for money?"

"No."

"Have you given her money…gifts, perhaps?"

"Not unless you count cake," Edward said tersely.

Ian Denholm sat back in his chair. "Could Mr. Kaufman be involved with someone else?"

"I beg your pardon?"

"It occurs to me that Mr. Kaufman might be happy for you to spend time with his wife because he's otherwise occupied. Of course that doesn't go to why he might kill Vogel, but it does speak to his character."

"But...that's...I don't know," he said in the end. "I barely know Kaufman. Generally speaking, we avoid one another."

"Were Mr. Kaufman and the deceased acquainted?"

Again, Edward was unable to say. "I could find out," he offered.

"What do you write, Mr. McGinnity?" Denholm asked suddenly as he leafed through a file on his desk.

"Novels."

"What kind of novels? You're not a crime-writer, are you?"

"Does it matter?"

"I find it does. I've represented writers before. The children's book writers believe in happy endings, the science fiction writers assume there's some sort of conspiracy at play, and the crime-writers take it upon themselves to investigate. None of these things are good ideas."

"What are you trying to say, Mr. Denholm?"

"Leave any investigation to me and the police, Mr. McGinnity."

"Rest assured, Mr. Denholm, I am not a crime-writer."

• • ● • •

Edward McGinnity turned as he always did to his notebook and pen for distraction. He called on Madeleine d'Leon to divert his frustration with Willow, his wounded brooding, and he found her on her knees, pulling weeds in the crisp damp of the morning garden. Her sleeves were rolled to the elbow and her collar turned up. She didn't look up.

"Maddie."

"The bruises were left by my bracelet." She dropped uprooted weeds into the bucket beside her.

He watched. "Talk to me, Maddie."

She turned her head. He stood with the early sun behind him, splaying its rays. His shadow fell on the ground before her, and Madeleine wondered if she was already too lost. How could something she imagined block the sun, how could a character cast a shadow, and why did she long for him?

"Are you angry with me, Maddie?"

"No, I'm angry with myself. I've started to believe my own lies."

"Lies?"

"That's what we trade in, we writers. We're crafters of lies. We call them novels or stories or narratives, but in essence they're a collection of lies…interesting, thrilling lies that make you laugh and cry, but in the end, still lies."

"Does that bother you?"

"No, it's what I do. But it's important to remember what's real, what's true."

"Perhaps telling lies is the only way to find the real truth."

Madeleine smiled. "That sounds literary. I'm not sure what it means, but it's exactly what one would expect a literary character to say. I'm quite pleased with how you're turning out."

He laughed that slow gentle laugh that was more a vocalised smile. And he studied her.

She stood, dusting off the grass which adhered to the wet patches on her knees. "What are you thinking?"

"I was wondering what to do next."

"Well, you need to look into Elliot Kaufman, his past, his associations. And you need to take another look at the security footage—in case there was something you missed."

"Or I could kiss you again, make love to you right here."

Madeleine stopped, startled. Had she wanted him to say that? The strange clenching ache that the night before had left on her skin had not yet dissipated.

"Do you want to?" she asked. The question was guileless, an honest curiosity about her own intentions as well as his.

"Yes, very much."

She blinked. This was all part of her fantasy, she supposed—that he would want her, value her. It seemed she could not even indulge in a simple erotic dream without embellishing and romanticising it. Even now he watched her intensely as if he were loath to miss even the slightest moment of her life.

Still, his proximity made her reckless.

He stroked her neck. "Did I do that?" He circled his thumb around each of the bruises. The question was more for himself than her, because of course he had. He wondered why. He had not done so consciously, but there would be a reason, some instinctive purpose which guided his pen to leave a mark on her body. Here, now, in the midst of this manuscript, he might have believed he was in love with Madeleine d'Leon, that he wanted her as more than a literary construct. Edward meant it when he said he wanted to make love to her, but he also wanted her to be more cautious.

And so she was.

"I slept on my bracelet." Madeleine held her hand up against the glare of the sun, displaying the denounced jewellery in the process. "It's getting too hot. I'm going inside to write." She bit her lip. "You're not going to get anywhere until you start investigating Geoffrey Vogel. The victim always holds the clue…you'd know that if you read."

"I do read." His protest was amused.

"Sorry—I meant if you read anything other than literary masterpieces. I'm afraid you don't solve crimes by learning about yourself."

He smiled. Madeleine's refusal to pay due homage to literary elitism was more charming than offensive. And it was not bad advice.

On Sidekicks

Edward closed his notebook and booted the laptop he'd purchased earlier that day. Whilst he wrote his novels longhand, he was by no means computer illiterate. He began with a basic search on Geoffrey Vogel, pulling up a biography, and various eulogies and articles about the murder. He read them all and followed threads within each site in the search for more information. But everything he found was media released and public related, sanitised. A veneer which hid goodness-knows-what, perhaps another veneer.

He had given up in frustration and was pouring himself a drink when Leith Henry called.

"I have some papers for you to sign," she said. "But I promised to take the kids to the park. I don't suppose you could meet me there, Ned?"

"Of course." He jotted directions and grabbed his jacket before heading out to meet his agent.

The park to which she'd directed him was a showpiece among modern recreational facilities. The equipment was new and made of recyclable material, designed in accordance with a prehistoric theme. Well-dressed children scaled climbing walls, descended slides, and swung with determined abandon as upwardly mobile parents hovered and encouraged from the surrounding trees. The ground beneath the play equipment was rubberised so that children bounced rather than fell.

Edward found Leith by the sandpit instructing her youngest on the finer points of sandcastle construction. The three-year-old watched on as she demonstrated sand compaction and tower placement. She upended a bucket and gently removed the mould. "See that, Tom, it's perfect. Now you try."

Tom lunged at the newly sculpted castle as if he were throwing himself upon a grenade. Sand flew in all directions and the castle was lost. Leith shrieked and expressed her disappointment in Tom's inability to use a sandpit properly. Somewhat unhelpfully, Ned applauded the three-year-old.

"Tom's a free spirit, Leith. He won't be confined by your sandpit rules."

Leith shook the sand from her hair. "William was never like this…he knew to find the corners first."

"What corners?"

"Of puzzles. Tom just takes any old piece and tries to jam the others into it."

"Hmmm. I'm afraid Tom's fast becoming my favourite. Where are your rule-abiding offspring?"

The agent pointed to the line-up of children waiting impatiently for their turn on the flying fox. She called names and two young Henries waved in response. With all three clearly in sight, she motioned Edward to a seat by the sandpit and, once she'd shouted reminders about hats and manners, she fished a folder from her large handbag. "I've tagged all the places that need your signature."

Edward retrieved a pen from his breast pocket and proceeded to sign. "And what is this?" he asked.

"The usual, in terms of foreign and collateral rights. An acknowledgement of your editorial control, an agreed marketing budget, and an escalation of royalties if the book sells more than fifty thousand copies."

"Sounds fair." Edward did not bother to read the documents himself. He trusted Leith to look after that sort of thing and, in any case, there was something else he wanted to discuss.

"Leith, what do you know about Geoffrey Vogel?"

"I heard he died."

"No, really, what do you know about his background?"

"Not much…he worked for a number of publishing houses as an editor. I suspect you're not the only writer who found his approach overbearing. Somehow he morphed into a critic, had a television show called *Arts Review* for a while. Most recently he reviewed for the *Herald*."

"What do you know about his personal life?"

Leith poked him. "Look at you, Sherlock!"

"I'm just trying to think this through," Edward replied. He felt vaguely embarrassed.

Leith smiled. "Afraid I can't help you, Ned. I haven't a clue." She paused to flutter her eyelashes appealingly. "Though I still want to be your quirky but loyal sidekick."

Edward sighed.

"I'm sorry," Leith said, still smiling. "But don't you think you're getting a bit Famous Five about this? I hate to sound like your agent, but shouldn't you be writing?"

"I am…I am writing."

"Good. Are you going to have something for me to read soon?"

"Soon. I guess I'll have plenty of time to write in prison."

"Don't be ridiculous, Ned. They don't let you write books in prison. You'll be busy breaking rocks and doing laundry."

Edward laughed.

"Go home and finish that manuscript. Let the police worry about Geoffrey Vogel."

"You're a terrible sidekick, you know."

"But I'm a brilliant agent. Stop messing about and write!"

Edward had every intention of doing as he was told. Madeleine could see that, feel that. Despite everything that was happening, the hero of her crime novel really just wanted to write. In the absence of Willow, she would need to prompt him within the story. Leith had been less than motivational, but then Leith was his agent and that was exactly what she would say. It was then Madeleine remembered the reporter from Channel Six.

Edward saw the business card on the hallstand as he came in. It was perhaps peculiar that he noticed it now when he'd missed it before, but Edward did not pause to think about that. He picked up the card that Peter Blake had left days earlier—the reporter had claimed friendship with Geoffrey Vogel. He wandered into the kitchen and called Peter Blake's number.

Madeleine cheered out loud. The sound startled her in the emptiness of the house. She'd had no idea that Peter Blake would have any further part to play in the novel when she'd first written him, but he was perfect here. It pleased her when this happened. She wondered if readers ever guessed that the coherence of her plots was often accidental.

"It's not, you know," Edward muttered as he hung up the phone after arranging to meet the reporter.

"What?"

"It's not accidental. Somewhere in your subconscious you have it all worked out, plotted, tied up. You shouldn't underestimate yourself."

Madeleine rolled her eyes. "Just go see the man."

Peter Blake was waiting in the beer garden of the inner-city tavern. He stood, though there were stools available, shifting his weight on the balls of his feet like a boxer awaiting the bell. He was in motion as soon as he saw Edward, going to the bar and collecting two glasses and a bottle of whisky, which he took to a table. Edward joined him there. The journalist lit a cigarette and poured two drinks, one of which he swigged straight away.

Refusing to cooperate with the unfolding cliché, Edward declined the whisky and ordered a coffee. Blake raised the second glass.

"I thought you'd want to come clean sooner or later," he said. "I'm glad you came to the realisation that I'd give you a fair hearing."

Edward responded cautiously. If Blake realised he wasn't going to get a confession, he might not be as forthcoming. "I have a few questions for you first."

"Why?" Blake took a recording device from his breast pocket and set it on the table.

Edward shrugged. "It's important to me to know a bit about Geoffrey Vogel. I barely knew him."

"Okay..." Blake said suspiciously. "And then we'll talk about what happened the night Geoff died?"

"Certainly."

"What do you want to know?"

"Did Vogel have a partner of some sort? Was he involved with anyone?"

"Not particularly. Geoff was a bit of a tart. He was just celebrity enough to mean there was always some ambitious young thing willing to keep him from becoming lonely."

"Weren't any of these ambitious young things upset when he decided to move on?"

"Is that what you're trying to tell me, McGinnity? That you were upset when he moved on from you?"

"Me?" Edward moved the bottle of whisky out of the way and stared at Blake. "What the—?"

"You're just the kind of strapping talent that he liked to take under his wing."

Edward paused. "You're saying Vogel was gay?"

"Gay, homosexual, queer...whatever you call it nowadays. It was an unofficial secret, but I would have thought it obvious."

It probably was, on reflection, but it hadn't before occurred to Edward. Flamboyant affectations were, after all, something of a tradition in the arts community.

Blake squinted at him. "You didn't know?" He sat back in his chair. "Well then, I guess this was more than a simple crime of passion."

"Maybe, maybe not." Edward forgot for a moment that Blake assumed he was there to confess. "Do you know who Vogel was more recently involved with, even briefly?"

"It's a long list," Blake said uneasily. "As I said, Geoff was a tart."

"Could you write the names down?"

"You want me to write you a hit list? Forget it, mate."

"Hit list, no. I just want to find out who might have had cause to—"

"Look, McGinnity, I know you topped Geoff. I just thought you might like a chance to tell the world why. You'll have to face a real trial, of course, but the sympathy of the media won't hurt your case."

"I didn't kill Geoffrey Vogel," Edward said slowly.

"That's not what the police believe."

"Whatever you think they believe, Mr. Blake, I have not been charged, and I'm telling you, I had nothing to do with Geoffrey Vogel's death."

"Then why are you here, Mr. McGinnity?"

"The lines of enquiry that the police seem to be following are, I believe, misdirected. I was hoping you might help me unearth some alternative lines."

Blake studied him, clearly disappointed. "What's in it for me?"

"You said Vogel was your friend. You'd be helping to bring his killer to justice."

Blake shrugged. "Perhaps friendship was an exaggeration. I wasn't Geoff's type."

"However this turns out, working with me will give you an exclusive, either as an investigative exposé which reveals the real killer, or an insight into the mind of the prime suspect."

"And what if you decide to do me in?"

Edward laughed. "You've been reading too many crime novels."

"You'll find crime fiction often holds a mirror to society," Blake warned, though he smiled now.

"Then we have a deal?" Edward offered Blake his hand, still feeling vaguely ridiculous. "Whatever happens, you have the scoop."

"Please don't say scoop." The reporter shook his head. "Yeah, okay, let's say we'll share information and I'll keep an open mind."

A Peace Offering

The yellow 1953 Vauxhall Cresta caught Madeleine's attention from the window of the tobacconist's shop. Still in its original box, among hookahs and silver flasks, it was positioned to beckon collectors. Writers were probably not in the proprietor's contemplation as a market. It wasn't that the model made her think of Edward, because she was always thinking of him now, but that she knew he'd like it.

"That's a very special piece," the tobacconist said on enquiry. "Rare in mint condition—which this one is." He put the box on the counter rather than allowing her to handle it. "I can let you have it for four hundred and sixty dollars."

Madeleine tried not to let the horror show on her face, though it was probably apparent in the way her shoulders drew back. Common sense told her that it was a ridiculous price for a toy. But she wanted so much now to give it to Edward.

"Is your husband a collector?" the tobacconist enquired, assessing her.

"No, but it isn't for him." Madeleine handed over her credit card.

She slipped the box into her bag, making sure it wasn't crushed by the flotsam of daily life which languished there, and hurried to meet her agent for lunch.

Leith was perched upon a stool at the sushi bar. She took her handbag off the stool she'd saved for Madeleine.

"Hello, Maddie…what are you looking so chirpy about?"

"A bit of retail therapy, that's all."

"Always worthwhile. How are you?"

"The novel's coming along well, I think."

"I asked about you, not your novel." Leith squeezed wasabi paste onto her dish.

"We're both fine," Madeleine opened a little fish-shaped container of soy sauce.

"Good." Leith selected a nori roll. "I hadn't heard from you in a while. I was a little worried."

"It hasn't been that long." Madeleine's brow wrinkled. Leith was not normally so easily concerned. She set down her chopsticks and met the agent's eye. "What gives?"

Leith sighed. "Hugh called me."

"Really? What about?"

"He's worried about you. He thinks perhaps you've been working too hard on this new novel."

"He said that?" Madeleine could hear the shrillness in her own voice. She tried consciously to moderate it. "Why does he think that?"

Leith patted her hand reassuringly. "He's worried that you spend so much time at the computer, that you rarely leave the house these days. He said you missed a couple of work meetings last week."

"I wasn't feeling well," Madeleine replied, "and they

weren't important meetings." She'd had a vague sniffle and the meetings weren't crucial.

"He's also concerned that you are not taking the Grand Oak Productions offer seriously."

"How does he even know about that?"

"I don't know. I thought you must have told him."

Madeleine shook her head...and then she remembered. "Tarquin called last week about the offer when Hugh was home. Perhaps he overheard." She frowned. "He didn't say anything."

"He thought perhaps you were making excuses so you could stay with the novel. Hugh all but begged me to insist you come to lunch—just to get you out of the house."

Madeleine could feel the flush rising on the back of her neck. "How dare he! Why didn't he just speak to me?"

"Calm down, honey. Hugh says the two of you are not communicating well, that you've withdrawn from him."

Madeleine could not speak. Hugh's complaints were not unfounded, but that did not prevent a defensive resentment lodging like a rock in her gut. It was heavy and hard. She took a breath and made her argument.

"Leith, I'm in the middle of a novel...and, yes, I'm immersed in my work, but no more so than I am with any other book. I don't leave the house because I like to work in my pyjamas and you can't do that at coffee shops or wherever it is Hugh wishes me to write. Damn! I can't believe Hugh is complaining that I work too hard—he's barely ever home!"

"He's a man, Maddie. They are not always fair or even reasonable. I told Hugh that each book has different demands...perhaps this one is taking more out of you."

"Each book is more challenging than the one before. It's why writers improve with experience."

"I know, Maddie. I didn't ask you here to plead Hugh's case, just to give you the heads-up that he might be feeling neglected."

Madeleine rolled her eyes and stabbed at a piece of sushi with her chopstick.

Leith screwed up her face. "It's kind of cute, really… he's jealous of your book. Just organise a romantic dinner or something, seduce him once or twice—he won't care how much you write after that. We can shop for some fox wear after lunch, if you like."

"Fox wear?"

"It's what Jase calls lingerie…"

"Oh, my God!"

"Seriously, Maddie, don't be cross that your husband misses you. I think there'd be more to worry about if he didn't feel a little put out."

Edward watched Madeleine carefully. He had written a woman who loved her husband. When he'd begun, that love had been simple, doubtless. And then he'd interfered.

Madeleine refused to see him. Refused to acknowledge the creeping confused sense of disloyalty. "Yes, of course. I'll try."

Hugh was home when Madeleine returned. It surprised her to find him so, but perhaps it was a slow day at the surgery. She grabbed her bags from the boot and headed inside.

"Hugh?"

"In the kitchen."

He was washing dishes.

"Good lord, you've been cooking!" Madeleine glanced at the stack of dishes on the sink.

"I got hungry. There's nothing left, I'm afraid. We might have to order out for dinner. What'd you buy?" He pointed at the shopping bag in her hand.

Madeleine squirmed a little. "New pyjamas."

"Well, you can never have too many, I suppose—not when you wear them day and night."

"I guess," Madeleine said, trying hard to ignore the note of criticism. "Shall I dry?"

"No, I'll just let it drain. Why don't you ask Jeeves to cook Chinese tonight, and I'll go in and pick it up?"

Madeleine nodded happily, reassured by the solid familiar presence of their private butler. Taking the restaurant menu down from the refrigerator door and to the phone, she spoke to Jeeves.

"Fifteen minutes," she announced as she hung up.

Hugh wiped his hands and grabbed her car keys. "I'll head out now. It'll be ready by the time I get there."

Madeleine took her bags into the bedroom while he was gone. Sitting cross-legged on the bed, she pulled out the little Vauxhall Cresta in its original box and placed it on the pile of books on her bedside table.

Edward's face was unreadable when he picked it up, extracting the car and examining it on the flat of his palm. "Jacob would have fought me for this," he said, running his finger over the pristine cardboard box. His brother had loved the older models and he'd cherished the distinctive boxes.

Madeleine hesitated then, began to doubt the impulse that had made her buy the yellow Vauxhall. Edward noticed. And he smiled, touched, by the tentative excitement in her eyes, the uncertainty in her lips. He, too, gave in to impulse and he kissed her, tenderly.

Madeleine felt her heart rise as he seemed to breathe her in. She allowed herself to linger in that kiss…a harmless fantasy. In time she pulled away. She could hear Hugh's car coming into the driveway.

She grabbed her shopping bags and slipped into the en suite to change, forgetting perhaps that Edward was in her head and not her bedroom. She donned the nightshirt she'd purchased as a compromise. It was not exactly fox wear but at least it was not flannelette. She tried to think about Hugh, to push Edward McGinnity away, to confine him to the pages of her manuscript so that she could be excited about her husband.

Edward observed her nervousness, as intrigued by how painful it was to watch—how much he didn't want her to return to the husband he'd created for her—as he was by her struggle.

He recognised that he was losing perspective, immersing himself in his own process to a level that might be delusional—dangerous, even. But how could he pull back now? How could he never know what might have happened? That Madeleine was affecting him, changing him was confronting, even frightening. But he was fascinated by the notion of a story truly told by both the writer and the protagonist. Perhaps this was the partnership that all writers sought, that he had never before completely achieved. Whatever the cause, the surge of possessiveness was unmistakeable.

"Maddie, don't."

"What?" Madeleine was startled. Did he say that? Was it simply what she wanted him to say?

"Maddie, I think you should be careful."

"Of Hugh?" she asked incredulously. "He's my husband."

"I don't trust him." Edward was unsure when and why he'd decided that…if in fact he had decided.

"Now you sound like a crime-writer," Madeleine laughed. "Perhaps he'll murder me and bury me under the roses."

"That's not what I meant."

"Maddie—dinner's getting cold!"

Hugh had placed the containers of stir-fried vegetables, honey chicken, and Singapore noodles on the table with a bundle of cutlery.

"I'll organise plates," Madeleine said, "unless you want to eat straight out of the containers?"

"It'd save washing up, which is the point of having Jeeves cook," Hugh replied.

"Let's hang on to plates as some last facade of civilisation." Madeleine moved to fetch dishes. There were two plates on the draining board, and two wineglasses as well as a couple of pots and utensils.

"Did you have someone call in for lunch today?" she asked as she set a plate in front of Hugh.

"No, just me on my own." He spooned half the noodles onto his plate and handed the container to his wife.

"There are two wineglasses on the sink."

Hugh's eyes narrowed. "Are you checking up on me again?"

"No. I was just wondering who came by."

"Nobody."

"Why would you use two wineglasses?"

"The first bottle I opened was corked. I used a fresh glass for the second."

"You don't usually drink wine at lunch," Madeleine said almost to herself.

"Well, I did today!" Hugh snapped. "It's the first day off I've had in months, I thought I was entitled." He pushed away his plate. "For God's sake, Maddie!"

"I'm sorry. I wasn't trying to—"

"Well, what the hell were you trying to do?"

"Nothing…I was simply making conversation. Let's just eat, okay?"

"I'm not hungry anymore."

"Please, Hugh, I'm sorry."

"I want you to see someone, Maddie. A professional."

"What…because I asked about lunch?"

Hugh stood. "You're depressed. You may not recognise it but I do. You rarely get dressed or leave the house, you spend every minute on that bloody computer, you talk about some figment of your imagination as if he were real. You've shut me out, you barely speak to me unless it's about him or unless you're accusing me of God-knows-what."

Madeleine recoiled, shocked by the way he saw things.

"You're avoiding the real world and calling it writing, Maddie!"

"Hugh, I'm not depressed…I'm just not. Maybe I am a little obsessed with this novel, but that's just the way I work. I'm sorry if I've shut you out—I haven't meant to."

"If you're sorry, then see someone. I have a colleague who specialises in this sort of thing. If you're not depressed, he'll be able to tell, and if you are, he'll be able to help."

"But I'm not—"

"I mean it Maddie. I'm at my wit's end. I love you more than anything in this world, but we can't go on like this."

Madeleine heard that he loved her, and it made her long for the way it had been. And so she had only to agree. What harm would it do? A psychiatrist would see she was not depressed and she would show Hugh that she cared what he thought, what he wanted. He would feel silly and apologise and things would be the way they were. And so she agreed.

He took her hand. "Thank you, Maddie. You'll see—it'll help."

They ate dinner then. For some reason, Madeleine felt shy now. Perhaps it was the knowledge that Hugh was seeing her differently, that he was scrutinising her. Knowing she should not mention her writing or anything connected to her writing, she was not sure what was left to say. She asked Hugh about his work, but he too seemed reluctant to speak of the surgery. So they talked about their meal, of Chinese food in general, then food, the modern obsession with cuisine, celebrity chefs, and then celebrity. In this way they filled the space with conversation. As they washed up the dishes they'd used, Madeleine remembered that there had been two plates as well as two glasses. She let it go.

They made love that night because not doing so seemed like it would hold too much significance.

Madeleine worked, wanting Hugh to find pleasure in her, wanting to bring back that first lust that they once thought would never wane, but which had given way to a kind of content familiar laziness. He seemed careful and, in the final throes, angry, thrusting into her with a battering fierceness, which might have been erotic but was not. And when they were finished, Madeleine told herself that they were both just trying too hard. As Hugh fell asleep, she turned to Edward.

Scrutiny

Edward had seen many counsellors and psychologists in the years after the accident. Earnest, harried professionals from the Department, who either cared too much or far too little, followed by the slick, excessively specialised private experts retained by Andy Finlay to testify in his case. Despite the differences, it wasn't difficult to conglomerate them into a single character, as they had become so in his memory—the result was a strangely removed, sexually ambiguous practitioner who reflected and summarised ad nauseum.

Edward called the physician Gerry McCauley and made him a man only so that he'd know which pronoun to use. Dr McCauley would, at the request of his old friend, Hugh Lamond, see Madeleine d'Leon on a bi-weekly basis.

Madeleine's eyes widened as she stepped into McCauley's large office. The red and gold seals of various universities and institutes formed an ordered constellation on the white facing wall. A single file sat on the desk, slim, closed. Madeleine presumed it was her file, newly opened. Two leather armchairs, placed at opposite ends of a Persian rug, were angled towards a studded couch. It was this that caught Madeleine's attention in particular. She had always thought the psychiatrist's couch a Hollywood myth.

"The divan is just so I can have a power nap at lunch," McCauley said smiling. His teeth were large and long—rather like a horse—and he held the smile for a beat too long. "You don't have to lie on it, I promise you... unless you want to, of course."

Madeleine shook his hand. "The armchairs look perfectly comfortable, Dr. McCauley." She smiled too, determined to demonstrate as quickly as possible, that she was not depressed.

He agreed and asked her to take her pick. She chose the seat furthest from the door so that he would not think she was keen to leave...which she was. He wrote a note.

He sat with one long leg draped over the other as he explained that their sessions would simply be "chats" giving her the opportunity to talk about anything she wanted...that she was simply to regard him as a sympathetic ear.

She nodded and he made a note.

Madeleine was tempted to ask him what he was writing, but she thought better of it. Instead she told him about her writing, her method such as it was, how that sometimes made her uncommunicative but did not mean she was depressed.

"So sometimes you don't feel like talking?" he said, jotting the fact down.

"No, it's not that. Sometimes I'm so caught up with what I'm writing, I forget to talk," Madeleine struggled to find the correct words. "It's like getting immersed in a good book and losing track of time. It's not that I don't want to talk, I just forget."

"Yes, of course I understand."

Madeleine wasn't sure that he did, so she tried to explain further. "I know Hugh thinks I'm depressed, but in some ways I'm happier than I've ever been."

"In some ways…what ways?"

"I don't know. I feel most myself when I'm writing."

"Why is that, do you think?"

"I'm not sure."

"Do you think you might use your writing to avoid confronting other aspects of your life?"

"What aspects?"

"How about you tell me?"

"I have no idea."

McCauley wrote a note. Madeleine responded to his silence. "There's really nothing in my life that I wish to avoid. Everything's perfect."

"Perfect?"

"Yes."

"I believe you and Hugh have been trying to have children. That you've suffered a number of setbacks."

"Did Hugh mention that?"

"It's on your medical file."

"I see."

"It's natural to mourn loss, Madeleine. Failing to do so leads to unresolved grief and, potentially, depression."

"I'm not depressed."

"Mental illness is quite difficult to self-diagnose, I'm afraid. It doesn't always manifest as melancholia."

"I'm not depressed."

McCauley made a note. "How about we just talk about how you're feeling, without worrying about labelling it. Tell me about this novel of yours."

Madeleine exhaled. Getting frustrated was only going to look like she was covering something up. Surely he'd be able to see she was perfectly lucid once he'd talked to her for a while. So she told him about her manuscript, the set-up, the victim, the murder, the investigation, and of course, Edward McGinnity. She discussed the tropes of crime fiction, the psychology of the genre, and the importance of finding a fresh angle.

McCauley showed particular interest in her protagonist, enquiring about character development, backstory, etcetera. He took detailed notes.

Though a little part of Madeleine baulked at talking about Edward, she was heartened by the fact that the psychiatrist seemed interested. Perhaps he was beginning to see that she was just an ordinary writer with only a very ordinary level of obsession. She began to feel confident. "I hope you're not planning to steal my idea," Madeleine laughed as McCauley turned the page and wrote some more.

He seemed a little alarmed for a moment, and then he too laughed. "No, no…but this is very interesting and I'm eager to learn more about young Edward McGinnity. Unfortunately, our time is up. Perhaps when you come to see me on Thursday."

"Oh." Madeleine had been hoping, expecting that after this session he would deem any further visits unnecessary. "I thought—"

McCauley leaned forward in his chair towards her. "What do you think if we keep meeting for a while to set Hugh's mind at ease? We can just talk about your books or anything else for which you need an objective sounding board. I've agreed to see you as a professional courtesy to Hugh, so there'll be no fees involved. I suspect knowing you have any support you may need, may help him deal with his own grief."

"His grief?"

"You've both suffered a loss…a number of losses."

"Of course…if you think it would help Hugh."

"I know it would." McCauley closed his notebook. "I'll see you at ten o'clock on Thursday, then."

• • ● • •

Edward hadn't used his gym membership in months. He preferred to run on the road or the beach rather than on some machine which simulated the road or the beach. About that, he'd not changed his mind, but he had remembered that Elliot Kaufman was also a member of Phytness Phyrst. In her more resentful moments, Willow complained that her husband spent more time perfecting his own body than he did those on his canvasses, though Edward noticed that the figures in Kaufman's work also seemed burdened with an excessive amount of muscle. It was that musing on Kaufman's artistic style that unearthed from indifference the realisation that Kaufman only painted men. His portraits, group compositions, even his crowd scenes were made up of solely men. It might not mean anything—perhaps it was just a stylistic quirk, some generalisation of humanity into mankind. But in the light of Peter Blake's revelations about Vogel, Edward wondered if it was something more fundamental. Was that the link between Kaufman and the dead man?

And so Edward McGinnity had started working out...or at least turning up to Phytness Phyrst in gym gear. It wasn't long before he spotted Kaufman at the bench press. Edward joined an army of joggers advancing upon personal goals via treadmills. From there he had a good view of the weights area from behind the phalanx of runners.

Kaufman called for someone to spot him. The man who obliged was gorillaesque in both stature and follicular abundance. He and Kaufman exercised together for a while, first at the weights and then with the punching bags. A couple of others joined them and though they seemed in earnest conversation, Edward could not tell if they were discussing anything more interesting than protein shakes.

The treadmill beeped to indicate that the maximum one-hour session would be over in five minutes. Edward skipped the warm down, surveying the gym for equipment that would put him unobtrusively within earshot of Kaufman and his companions. He was just about to take his place at a rowing machine when the men he was watching walked out. Edward grabbed his towel and followed.

The saunas were housed at the back of the gym and were going through a phase of unpopularity. A year ago it had been necessary to book them a week in advance. Now Kaufman and the others were able to walk in without notice. Even so, they all chose to use the same sauna room.

Edward waited several minutes before peering through the small glassed porthole into the room. He'd braced himself to witness some kind of illicit orgy. Strangely, there was no condensation on the window, no steam to cloak further what transpired behind the door. Kaufman stood on a stepped wooden bench with a towel around his waist, parted at the side, his eyes clenched closed and his face contorted into a grimace. The hirsute man, also wearing only a towel, was bent over a gym bag. He removed a vial, the contents of which he extracted into a hypodermic needle. He held the needle to the light, tapped it twice and plunged it into Kaufman's thigh. The other two men stood watching with their arms folded. Then, in turn, each stepped up to take Kaufman's place.

Drugs. Edward shook his head. Of all the uncomplimentary things he had thought about Kaufman, he had never suspected the artist of being an addict. The vice did not interest him particularly, unless it was being used as foreplay of some sort.

Certainly the men in the sauna seemed to be displaying their bodies to each other, flexing, comparing musculature, but in a way that was more narcissistic than homoerotic. And then it occurred to Edward. Steroids. He cursed, irritated that he had wasted time and effort chasing down something so facile and irrelevant to Geoffrey Vogel.

Perhaps he spoke more loudly than he intended, because Kaufman looked up. There was a split second when both men realised they had been discovered, and then, a call to action. Edward moved quickly, making his way hastily back towards the gym proper, knowing

Kaufman and his comrades would have to put on more than towels in order to follow him.

"Ned! I say, hallo!" Adrian Barrington caught up with him as he passed the treadmills. He was attired for conspicuous exercise in a Nike tracksuit and running shoes which were so white they produced a glare. "I didn't know you were a member here."

"Will bought me a membership last Christmas," Ned said glancing behind him.

"Oh, good show…I don't suppose you're interested in a personal trainer. It might be easier to let James go if I found him another client first."

"To be honest I don't think I'm a gym person, Al. This is the first time I've been in months." Edward tried to manoeuvre past Barrington.

"A recalcitrant, eh? It sounds to me like you *need* James," Barrington moved in front of Edward again, determined to make a sale.

The door leading to the sauna rooms opened. Elliot Kaufman, in track pants, a t-shirt, and untied shoes came through it into the hallway.

"I'm afraid I really must be going," Edward said attempting to sidestep past the agent. "I'm sorry, I can't take James off your hands, Adrian."

"Oh, I say, there's Elliot. You've met Willow's beloved husband, haven't you? Of course you have." Barrington beckoned Kaufman, who hesitated now.

"Kaufman and I have already run into each other today." Edward finally slipped past the enthusiastic art dealer.

"Drink—let's have a drink soon," Barrington called after him.

Edward waved apologetically as he wove through the equipment towards the side exit. He looked back to see that Barrington had quite obligingly delayed Elliot and the men with him in his desperation to offload his personal trainer. Kaufman was not taking it well. His face was dark and aggressive, his stance agitated. Barrington seemed disdainful, if anything. And so Edward McGinnity made his escape.

He next saw Kaufman emerging from Phytness Phyrst just as he was pulling the Mark II out of the parking lot.

Edward half-expected the four men to jump into a car, and give chase, but they didn't. Of course they wouldn't. This was real life not pulp fiction. Real people did not get involved in car chases. "Real people don't wander about gyms spying, either," he muttered to himself. "What the hell did I think I was doing?"

"What you had to," Madeleine said.

"I didn't have to do anything, Maddie," Edward replied, happy to have her company. "I'm not a detective."

"Nobody's asking you to wear a deer hunter and cape."

"No, but I really don't know what I'm doing."

"Do any of us?"

"That's a bit philosophical for a crime-writer."

"You'd be wise not to underestimate us."

"I have no doubt."

Madeleine regarded him fondly. "Crime-writers specialise in life and death, in justice and retribution. What could be more philosophical?"

"Does Veronica Killwilly consider the greater questions of existence while she tracks down killers, then?" he asked. She noticed the creases in the corners of his eyes, laugh lines which gave away a smile not yet visible.

She shoved him. "No. Ronnie isn't quite so dull."

Edward felt the gentle impact of her arm against his. His mother would push him like that when he was being cheeky, when the joke was just between the two of them. It occurred to him that he was projecting his memories again...perhaps that's why he found it so easy to love Madeleine d'Leon. He glanced at her, in the car beside him. He was intrigued by her, seduced by her and he was not entirely sure why. Silently he cursed Vogel and Kaufman and Bourke for keeping him from sinking into her story, from languishing in the woman he'd conjured.

He pulled into his own driveway determined to write, to ignore the mayhem his own life had become for a while.

• • ● • •

Hugh did not ask Madeleine about her session with the psychiatrist, but somehow he made it clear that he was pleased with her. He brought home flowers and a frozen Black Forest cake from the Ashwood general store. Madeleine felt both irritated and stupidly gratified by his approval. She thanked him for the flowers and put the cake out to defrost. They were so careful with each other nowadays. It was almost a relief when he announced he had to return to the surgery.

"Save me some cake," he said grabbing his briefcase.

Madeleine wasn't quite sure what to say...too scared, lest it start a fight, to ask what was so important. The thought of another quarrel was exhausting—the peace between them so brittle and fragile.

"I'll try to be home by eleven, but don't worry if I'm not. I've got a lot of paperwork to get done."

Madeleine started on the cake whilst it was still partially frozen. She sat alone in the kitchen sucking cake and thinking about the two plates and two glasses that she and Hugh had fought over a couple of days before. The second glass he'd explained, but not the second plate.

Once upon a time she would have asked him, told him that she wished he'd come home, that she didn't understand what was happening to them. But that time was once. Past. Madeleine wondered if she and Hugh would ever get back the closeness they'd known…the ability to say anything, speak frankly, a confidence in the other's kindness that they'd taken for granted and forgotten to protect. She was aware that she loved Hugh less now, and it frightened her. How could something that was as constant and fierce as the sun be suddenly less? It made her feel like the sun, too, would one day diminish and the world would grow cold.

For a time Madeleine cried in the privacy of her empty house with only Edward McGinnity to see. She was aware of him and for some reason she was comforted by the fact that he remained—that, in her petty misery, he stayed.

"Maddie," he said, gently pushing a damp wisp of hair back from her face. "I'm sorry you're so sad."

Her smile was watery and flickering. "You think I'm depressed, too," she said, trying to hold back fresh tears.

He shook his head. He kissed her hand. "I think you're sad. And I think Hugh's a bastard."

Edward was more surprised by his own words than Madeleine.

"It's not Hugh's fault." Her defence was reflexive. "I've been...preoccupied."

He let it go. "So what now, Maddie?"

"I'll write I suppose," she said quietly.

Edward nodded. Her hand still in his, he moved towards the bedroom. "Come, spend the evening with me."

A Thickening

The knocking had begun some time before Edward McGinnity registered it enough to stop what he was doing. He cursed, placing the little Vauxhall Cresta onto the coffee table and recapping his fountain pen before answering the door.

"Detective Bourke."

"Good afternoon, Mr. McGinnity. May we come in?"

Edward stood back to admit Bourke and O'Neil, who typically said nothing. "What can I do for you, Detectives?"

"Where were you this morning, Mr. McGinnity?"

Edward frowned. Tragedy had granted him freedom of movement earlier than most, thrust him young into self-determination. And so the intrusiveness of the question irked him unreasonably and he reacted in a way that may have appeared evasive. "What is this about, Detective?"

"We've received a complaint from Mr. Elliot Kaufman."

"I see."

"Mr. Kaufman alleges that you are stalking him."

"Stalking?" Edward scoffed. "Why would I stalk him?"

"Mr. Kaufman says you are obsessed with his wife. He is concerned he may end up like Geoffrey Vogel."

"Oh, for the love of—"

"Were you following Mr. Kaufman this morning?"

"Mr. Kaufman and I happen to be members of the same gym."

"And is it your habit to attend this gym on Wednesday mornings?"

"Well…no, not really."

"Can I ask why you chose to go this morning?"

"I wanted to exercise."

"Mr. Kaufman says he's never seen you at Phytness Phyrst before."

"I'm flattered he's noticed." Edward shrugged. "I'm still recovering from the assault, Detective. I thought it would be more sensible to exercise in a monitored environment rather than running on the beach. I don't suppose you've had any progress finding the men who broke in here?"

"No, I'm afraid we have not, Mr. McGinnity?"

"I see." Edward decided to take the offensive. "Since you're here, Detective Bourke, I'd like to report a theft."

"You've been robbed, Mr. McGinnity?"

"Yes, I have. I did mean to report it when I first noticed, but circumstances got away from me."

"What exactly has been taken, Mr. McGinnity?"

"A 1955 Mercedes Gull Wing, a black Model T Ford, and a racing green Aston Martin."

Bourke stared at him. "You have a single car garage, Mr. McGinnity. Where exactly did you keep these cars?"

Edward pointed out the kilned-glass bowl which held his collection.

"You're reporting the theft of toys?"

"Models, collectibles. Yes."

"Are you sure you did not simply misplace them, Mr. McGinnity?"

"I'm certain, they were in that bowl before you took me in for questioning…while my house was being searched."

"What are you suggesting, Mr. McGinnity?"

"Nothing really, Detective. It is interesting, though, don't you think?"

O'Neil's skin looked damp. He spoke for the first time in Edward's recollection. "Do you have any evidence that these toys existed, Mr. McGinnity?"

"Now, what are *you* suggesting, Detective?" Edward demanded frostily.

"I wonder, Mr. McGinnity, if you are trying to cast doubt on the evidence gathered during the search of your property by alleging some form of impropriety."

"Now that you raise the possibility, Detective…" Edward returned calmly.

Madeleine smiled. Finally Edward McGinnity was sounding like a crime fiction hero.

O'Neil cleared his throat. "We'll look into it, Mr. McGinnity. Perhaps they were simply taken for testing… fingerprinting and the like."

Bourke looked at his colleague strangely.

"Unfortunately," Edward continued, "the models weren't noted on the list of evidence. It seems a little odd that you would have taken three cars only."

"That might have been an oversight. We'll check."

"I'd appreciate that, Detective."

Bourke tried to claw back some power. "Allow me to caution you, Mr. McGinnity, that it is a crime to intimidate or interfere with a witness."

"A witness...oh, you mean Kaufman. What did he witness?"

"Mr. Kaufman is seeking an apprehended violence order against you, Mr. McGinnity. Perhaps it would be better if you returned to running on the beach."

Edward frowned. It would probably serve no purpose to tell Bourke about what he'd witnessed in the sauna. "Fine."

• • ● • •

Edward phoned his lawyer when the detectives finally left. Recalling their last conversation on the matter of his investigation, Edward cast the encounter as coincidental. Ian Denholm was not fooled and less than pleased.

"I'll look into this apprehended violence order," he said curtly. "You stay away from Kaufman. The best way to help yourself, Mr. McGinnity, is not to!"

Edward did not defend or excuse himself. After all, he couldn't very well tell his lawyer that his actions had been at the urging of an imaginary crime-writer.

Even so, he called Peter Blake the moment he'd finished with Denholm. He told him what he had seen.

"So what are you saying, McGinnity? Kaufman uses steroids...so what?"

"Don't anabolic steroids make you more volatile? More likely to throw someone down a flight of stairs in a fit of pique?"

"Perhaps...but it's hardly a causal link. He's still got to have reason to enter the stairwell with Vogel and to fall out with him. Kaufman, by virtue of the steroids, may be more likely to lose it than you, but that's not to say you're not capable of losing it. Do you get me?"

"Yes…but I didn't—"

"And he says he didn't. Look, McGinnity, it was a good try, but steroids don't connect Kaufman to Vogel."

"Blast!" Edward murmured.

Blake's voice was amused. "Before this is all over, I'll teach you to swear properly."

Madeleine's head tilted as she pondered this last small exchange. Why didn't Edward McGinnity swear? For a man his age it was odd.

Edward seemed stricken when she asked. For a moment she thought he wouldn't answer. And then.

"I swore at my mother in the car," he said quietly. "I can't remember why…but I remember telling her to fuck off. I remember the look on her face in the rearview mirror, my father turning and then the bridge gave way. It turned out to be the last thing I said to her…to them. I can't swear without thinking about that, so I don't."

Madeleine put aside her laptop and reached out for him. "Oh, Ned, you were a child."

He flinched. Madeleine could see his memories now and she too blanched at the horror and confusion, the sudden onset of apocalypse, which seemed to have been ignited by a flash of teenage rebellion. And, as much as they both knew, there was no connection between the swearing and what followed, the incidents were there, forever seared together. There was nothing Madeleine could do and so she offered him her arms instead and when he fell into her embrace she rocked him like a child.

• • ● • •

"I'm a psychologist," Leith said shaking her head. "Couldn't you just tell Hugh you're seeing me?"

"I tried that. He said it would be unethical for you to treat me. I don't know, Leith. It's probably my fault." Madeleine shrugged. "I have been more involved in my work than usual. Sometimes I wonder if making me see someone is Hugh's way of dealing with his own feelings."

"He thinks he can be counselled vicariously?"

Madeleine laughed. "It sounds silly when you say it like that."

"That's because it is silly. Tell him to man-up and get his own therapist!"

"It does seem to make him feel better," Madeleine said still smiling. "We haven't been fighting as much. It's not such a big deal. If my talking to Dr. McCauley makes him happy…"

Leith peered at her.

"Forget Hugh. Are you happy, Maddie?"

Madeleine had told McCauley that she was the happiest she'd ever been. At the time she'd said it defensively, but, on some level, it was true. Writing Edward McGinnity, spending her thoughts and her time with Edward McGinnity, was exhilarating. She had but to think of his touch and…Leith noted the blush, the distant brightness in her client's eyes. "Oh, I see. The fox wear worked then."

"No! It wasn't that!"

Leith stirred her half-strength, soy milk decaf with her brow arched and her lips pursed. It was her triumphantly sceptical face. "Of course, it wasn't. There was nothing foxy about that nightshirt thing. But clearly you succeeded, despite it."

Madeleine rolled her eyes. There didn't seem any point in explaining, nor any way she could, really. How could she tell Leith about making love to Edward… about fantasies that made sex with her husband seem about as intimate and rudimentary as washing dishes?

The agent laughed. "You're being very coy! Still, I'm glad things are getting better for you and Hugh." She dug into her briefcase. "I have some good news for you. I pitched your new novel to Mereton Harcourt Publishing. They loved the first chapters and are anxious to see the full manuscript."

"Mereton Harcourt…" Madeleine was startled. The publishing house was large, one of the few remaining multinational operations. The news should have elated her. "I'm nowhere near finished, Leith…and then I'll have to redraft—"

"Rubbish—you never rewrite. Anyway, they'll understand it's a first draft."

"I don't know…"

"This is not the time for a crisis of confidence. Just put your head down and write. I told them we'd have a working draft to them in a month."

"A month? Are you out of your—?"

"You'll be fine, Maddie. Mereton Harcourt would be a great move. They're already talking about releasing simultaneously in the UK and U.S. This may just be your chance at the big-time."

"But I haven't finished the manuscript."

"Just try. If it doesn't work, I'll think of something. But promise me you'll try."

Madeleine sighed. How could she explain that she didn't want to finish this manuscript, that she wasn't ready to finish with Edward McGinnity? "Okay, I'll try…but I can't promise."

"That's good enough for me," Leith said, relieved. "Hugh will just have to share you with young Edward for a while."

● ● ● ● ●

Madeleine climbed into the freshly made bed, enjoying the feeling of cool clean sheets against her bare legs. She made a note to praise Hugh for this small act of domestic kindness. As much as he did do an equitable share of the housework, Hugh seemed to need his efforts acknowledged, applauded. He'd announce that he'd done the dishes, or mopped the floor or vacuumed, and wait expectantly for commendation. In the beginning it had irritated Madeleine, but now she found it amusing…teased him for it. Even so, she had never known Hugh to attend to the bed. He appeared to believe the linen fairy visited once a week to change the sheets. Madeleine had only remade the bed herself with clean linen two days before. Perhaps Hugh, too, was making an effort.

She gathered the pillows behind her and booted the laptop, smiling as the manuscript came up on the screen, enjoying the fluttering in her breast as she read his name. Just his name seemed to call out a secret intimacy from the page. Someday people would read what she'd written, but they would never know about her and Edward—never know him as she did, never feel him as she did. That belonged to her.

Edward was prepared for Willow's fury. What he was not ready for was her refusal to believe him. He had wrestled with whether to tell Willow about what he had seen. He had decided that she needed to know, needed to be warned, and some part of him suspected that Elliot Kaufman was more involved in events than they knew.

"How dare you!" she shouted. "How dare you try to excuse your behaviour by making up something so stupid!"

"Why is it stupid, Will? You say yourself that Elliot spends ridiculous amounts of time at the gym, he's built like a Besser brick, he's got a one-inch fuse and I saw him injecting." He took her by the shoulders and looked into her face. "I just want you to be careful…I don't think he's safe…"

She shook off his hands. "You're a liar, Ned! You're trying to turn me against my husband!"

"Yes, I am. I'm trying to make you see sense."

"In your own interests, not mine! I thought we could be friends, Ned, but clearly you're too immature, too selfish for that!" Willow's eyes were bright and livid. "You may consider that Elliot's AVO applies equally to me. Don't come near me, Ned. We're not friends anymore. I don't trust you anymore!"

He grabbed her arm as she turned to leave. "Will, please."

"Let go of me!" she shouted.

"Not until you listen."

She struggled. The security alarm went off. Willow screamed. The door, which Edward had failed to lock after he'd admitted the artist, flew open and Elliot

Kaufman charged in, swinging. Edward let go of Willow to defend himself. Somehow the kilned bowl was knocked off the coffee table and Matchbox cars flew in every direction. Elliot threw himself on Edward, yelling, "Let her go, you murdering bastard!"

Kaufman's fist caught Edward's jaw almost accidentally, for the punch was thrown wildly. Edward fought back and Kaufman reacted like an enraged bull, charging unthinkingly with his head down. Both men ended up on the floor. With the alarm and Willow's screams, it took Edward several moments to register that Kaufman too was screaming. Then he saw the blood.

Edward rose to his knees trying to make sense of what was happening. The kilned bowl had broken, his notebooks and pens lay amongst the fragments of glass. Kaufman rolled onto his side, choking and gurgling. A fountain pen was embedded in his throat.

"No!" Edward shouted as Kaufman grabbed the pen. Too late. Kaufman pulled the pen from his neck and with it came blood, spurting from his carotid with the pump of his heart. Moving quickly, Edward slammed his hand on the wound and pressed. Kaufman wheezed, flailing weakly.

"Get away from him!" Willow screamed, striking out at Edward. He fended her off without taking his hand from Kaufman's neck.

She clawed at him, screaming, crying, desperate to protect her husband. If the police hadn't arrived, she might have prevailed. As it was, the police pulled Edward McGinnity off anyway, but then there were at least paramedics on hand to take his place as a stauncher of blood. Willow was hysterical and Edward was dripping with Kaufman's blood when they arrested him.

Even as they took him away, he tried to reason with Willow. To explain. She would not hear him, clinging to the side of the gurney that bore Elliot Kaufman into the ambulance.

Madeleine paused, unsure. The scene had taken a turn she had not expected. Some part of her wanted to help Edward, to rescue him. The other part was a writer. She pondered whether Elliot Kaufman would die. There had been so much blood.

She decided to stop writing for a while so that the story had time to work itself out. Climbing out of bed, Madeleine smoothed the covers tautly back into place. The made bed gave her a ridiculous feeling of satisfaction. That Hugh had made it for her seemed such an intimate gesture. It made her feel warm, excited that perhaps everything was returning to normal.

She wondered what her newly domestic husband had done with the sheets. They were not in the hamper. Perhaps he'd already put them in the washing machine. In a sudden need to reciprocate, Madeleine decided she should hang them out. There was something wonderfully normal about hanging washing on the line. And then she'd bake.

"You'll just have to wait, Ned," she said, plugging the laptop in to recharge. "Until I figure things out a little."

Edward watched her thoughtfully. He was strangely touched by how small a thing it took for Hugh Lamond to call her back to him. How easy it was for her to believe in him.

Madeleine found the old sheets in the washing machine, but sadly, the cycle had stalled. The appliance automatically shut off when the load was too large. Madeleine opened the machine's door to remove some of the contents, wondering what the good citizens of Ashwood would think if they knew that the successful operation of a washing machine was beyond their revered doctor. She pulled out the sheets which had been bundled in without emptying the previous load. The stain was impossible not to notice. Large, still bright red, though it had started to brown a little at the edges. Blood. Madeleine gasped, dropping the sheet in horror.

For several minutes she could not touch it, and then, steeling herself she checked it again. Surely it was blood. Partially dried now but thick. The top sheet and pillow cases were also smeared with the dark red stain. What had happened? Hugh must have cut himself somehow—rather badly. This was more than a shaving nick. But he couldn't be too badly injured. He had stopped to strip and make the bed. She was confused…worried, bewildered, and in the pit of her stomach a cold knot of suspicion. About what, she wasn't sure.

It occurred to her that the blood might not be Hugh's. No! That was absurd. This was not a story. There would be some mundane explanation. Still, Madeleine baulked at washing the sheets.

She gathered the soiled linen and sealed it in a garbage bag. For a while she paced, and then she went out to her car and shoved the bag into the spare tyre cavity of the boot.

Edward handed over his bloody clothes. They gave him a set of overalls to wear instead. Prison-issue, possibly. And they took photographs of the blood on his hands, his chest, his face, dozens of photographs. Edward wondered if Elliot Kaufman had died. He was having trouble concentrating on what was happening. Jumbled flashes of blood and screaming…the accident. He retreated to Madeleine's story only to come back to blood. And he felt sick.

Ian Denholm arrived. He shouted at Bourke about shock and appropriate medical care and then there were doctors. "I'm not hurt," Edward said vaguely, as they examined him. He told himself that the pain was a memory. Ian Denholm sat beside him in the interrogation room. Edward asked about Elliot Kaufman. Was he dead? Bourke would tell him nothing at first, and then O'Neil came in and took his partner aside.

"Mr. Kaufman is in surgery," he said. He spoke to Denholm. "We're going to hold your client until we've spoken to the victim and Ms. Meriwether."

"Why?" Denholm asked.

"Your client was involved in an altercation in which Mr. Kaufman was critically injured, Mr. Denholm," Bourke replied. "Surely why is self-evident."

"I'd like to talk to my client, Detectives," Denholm said brusquely. "And then we will discuss how long you may detain him."

Bourke shook his head but he got up to leave. O'Neil followed suit.

"Okay, what happened?" Denholm asked when they were alone.

Edward told him as best he could. "Will and I were arguing, Kaufman came charging in throwing punches, the alarm went off…"

"So Kaufman attacked you?"

"Not very competently, but yes."

"And you stabbed him in self-defence."

"I didn't stab him at all—he fell on the coffee table… my fountain pen was on it. It must have embedded in his neck. The fool pulled it out. I was trying to stop him from bleeding to death when the police arrived."

"Well, what the hell are they holding you for then?"

"I honestly don't know."

Denholm paced about the room for a while. Finally he stopped and sat down.

"Edward, I'm going to see what I can find out. Will you be all right for a few minutes?"

"Yes, of course."

"Don't speak to anyone until I return. If anyone tries to question you while I'm gone, demand your lawyer and say nothing else."

Edward nodded slowly. "I need to speak to Willow."

"Even if that were possible, I don't want you to speak to anyone until I return. Is that understood?"

"Yes. Fine. I'll just sit here."

"Good man, I won't be too long."

Madeleine sat on the table as Ian Denholm left the interview room. She rested her feet on a chair, her elbows on her knees and gazed at Edward with that mixture of curiosity and compassion.

He smiled faintly. "I'm not supposed to speak to anyone."

"I don't count." She offered him her hand almost shyly. "Are you okay, Ned?"

"I wasn't hurt." He pressed her hand to his cheek.

"You saved his life."

"So he'll live?"

Madeleine stopped. "I don't know."

"What are you doing, Maddie?"

"I don't know that either."

"The blood…"

"You did what you could, Ned."

"You're a crime-writer, Maddie. You can't ignore the blood."

She swallowed. "You're not a crime-writer."

He closed his eyes but the blood was still there, and the screaming he remembered wasn't Kaufman's. "I wish I could ignore it. I wish I could forget it."

"I'm so sorry, Ned." Madeleine's throat was tight. Her art was to torture this man, her instinct to protect him.

He tried to reach her, to give her the courage to see what she'd hidden in the boot of her car. "It's not the worst thing, Maddie—to be alone."

"You're not alone, Ned. Not now. I'm here. I won't leave."

Edward kissed the palm of her hand. He was strangely elated, comforted, by the idea. Madeleine d'Leon couldn't be taken away.

• • ● • •

Madeleine got dressed before Hugh returned home. She wasn't entirely sure why she did, nor why she remade the bed, removing any sign that she'd spent the afternoon in it with Edward McGinnity. And she made shortbread because Hugh loved shortbread and it was one of the few things she could make well.

"Something smells nice," he said, dropping his jacket over a chair. He looked at the tray of freshly baked biscuits. "Can I have one?"

"Of course. I made them for you."

He smiled. His old smile. The one she knew. "What's the occasion? I didn't forget an anniversary, did I?"

"The fact that you were brave enough to ask means you know you didn't," Madeleine replied. "No, I thought that since you were going all domestic god on me, I should try to do the homemaker bit too."

"I beg your pardon?"

"You made the bed."

"Oh, that. Jeeves isn't doing beds anymore. Something about the butler's award. Bloody unionised servants." He grabbed two shortbread biscuits and headed out to the laundry.

"What happened to the sheets?" he asked. "I threw them in the washing machine."

"I hung them out when I came home. They're back in the linen cupboard now," Madeleine said, hoping he wouldn't look.

"Goodo." Hugh strode back into the kitchen. He seemed more relaxed than Madeleine has seen him in a long while. Fleetingly, she wondered if it was relief. "Bacon and eggs for dinner?" he asked.

She nodded. "Sure."

Hugh didn't go back into the office that evening. Instead, they watched television, a movie, and two sit-coms, and ate shortbread dunked in tea. And Madeleine remembered how happy they had once been.

When finally they retired, Madeleine pressed close to him, her leg rubbing a quiet invitation against his. They talked about politics, the most recent skirmish between parties, then Hugh reminded her that she had an appointment with Dr. McCauley the following day, and rolled over to sleep. For a while, Madeleine listened to his breathing. Only when the rhythm slowed to a gentle snore did she accept that he was really asleep, that he intended nothing more. The disappointment was humiliating in itself. She wasn't sure what she'd expected, but even as he lay beside her, she felt abandoned. And sleep would not come.

Madeleine slipped out of bed and into the drawing room where she found her laptop and the company of Edward McGinnity.

• • ● • •

It was not yet nine in the morning when Madeleine knocked on her father's door. Her grandmother answered in a dressing gown. "Ahhh, Harijini…come in, come in Pu-thaa. I'm still in my housecoat." The old woman smoothed her long grey plait. "Has something happened?"

"No, Aach-chi, I have an appointment later. I just wanted to see Dad first."

"He's drinking his tea. Come, come, shall I make you something to eat?"

"I don't suppose you're making dosa, Aach-chi?" Madeleine asked, knowing her grandmother would now do so, and that the pancakes would take a while to prepare. She wanted to speak to her father alone.

"Hello, Dad." Madeleine kissed her father and took the chair beside him. He poured her a cup of tea.

"What brings you here, Madeleine? How is Hugh?"

"Hugh's fine, Dad. I need your help with something I'm writing."

The old man beamed. He loved being involved in his daughter's books.

"It's a bit sensitive," she warned. "Do you know a doctor who could test a bloodstain for me?"

"A bloodstain?"

"Yes, it has to do with something I'm working on, but I can't really tell you much more. I have a bloodstained sheet that I need tested."

"Tested—for what?"

The sizzle of dosa being fried in a well-oiled pan came from the kitchen as Madeleine tried to explain. "What they can easily tell me...blood type, whether it's human, that sort of thing, and where it might have come from."

"What has this to do with your writing?"

"It's kind of an experiment. Do you know anyone, Dad?" Madeleine knew the Sri Lankan expatriate community was full of doctors, most of whom had their tax returns done by her father. She pulled the sheet out of her bag, folded, wrapped in plastic.

"Is this legal?" her father asked, alarmed.

"Yes, of course. It's not from a crime scene," she said, with almost complete certainty. "If you could find someone who was willing to test it and write down exactly what they did to test it, then I could recreate the process in my story." Madeleine didn't need or want an account of the process, but it was the only thing she could think of which would make the request seem vaguely related to her writing.

"Asoka Wickramaratne runs a laboratory. I'll ask him if he can do something."

"Thank you, Dad."

"Madeleine, where did you get this cloth?"

"An informant," she said. "I really can't say any more."

"Has someone been injured?"

"I hope not. Will you just do this for me, Daddy? No questions. It's important."

Elmo Dhanusinghe sighed, but he agreed. His daughter was a lawyer—he accepted that she knew what she was doing, however odd the request seemed. "You look tired, Madeleine."

"I've been working a lot," she said. "I'll sleep in a bit when this book is finished."

Elmo sighed. "I think this will be the book."

"I think so, too," Madeleine said, not because she believed or even wanted it to be true, but because it made her father happy to think so.

Ian Denholm returned with Bourke and O'Neil. Denholm took the seat beside Edward, the detectives sat opposite.

"How's Kaufman?" Edward spoke to his lawyer.

Bourke replied. "Mr. Kaufman is out of surgery, but it will be a few hours before we can talk to him."

"I see."

"Ms. Meriwether has, however, given a statement. Mr. Denholm has convinced us that it might be time to take yours."

Edward glanced at Denholm. The lawyer nodded. "Go ahead, Ned. It's time to set the record straight."

Edward answered Bourke's questions, detailing and explaining the events which resulted in the hospitalisation of Elliot Kaufman.

"So you claim you were trying to render assistance to Mr. Kaufman?" Bourke asked.

"There was blood everywhere. I was trying to put pressure on the wound."

"And what was Ms. Meriwether doing at this time?"

"She was trying to pull me off."

"Why?"

"I suppose she didn't realise I was trying to help him."

"Why would she think you were attacking her husband?"

"She was hysterical."

"Would it surprise you to know, Mr. McGinnity, that Ms. Meriwether says in her statement that you stabbed Mr. Kaufman with your fountain pen?"

That it surprised him was obvious. Edward pulled back from the interview table shocked, puzzled. He shook his head. "She couldn't have said that."

O'Neil pushed across a copy of Willow Meriwether's signed statement. Edward scanned it quickly at first, and then slowly as if a careful reading would change its meaning. He pushed the paper back. "She couldn't have seen that. It's not what happened."

"Why would she lie, Mr. McGinnity?"

"I don't know…maybe she's confused. It all happened so quickly."

"Could it be that you're confused, Mr. McGinnity?"

"No."

"Then you are lying."

"No."

Denholm intervened. "It seems to me, gentlemen, that you have nothing other than the unsubstantiated allegation of a hysterical young woman on which to detain my client."

"Your client's fingerprints were on the fountain pen, Mr. Denholm."

"It was his pen. He used it earlier today. And surely if my client had plunged the pen into Mr. Kaufman's neck you would expect his palm and not his fingerprints."

"Have you examined the security footage?" Edward asked the detectives suddenly.

"What security footage?"

"The security system…my agent had it installed after the break-in. Every room in my house is monitored."

Bourke made a note. "We'll look into that. In the meantime, can you tell us what you and Ms. Meriwether were arguing about?"

Edward hesitated. "I was informing Ms. Meriwether about one of her husband's vices. She didn't want to hear it."

Bourke glanced at his colleague. O'Neil raised his brow. Clearly they had made some assumptions about the nature of the vice. Edward didn't bother to disillusion them.

"Why?" Bourke asked.

"Because he's her husband, I expect."

"I meant why did you feel the need to tell her? Surely, it was between them?"

"I suspected that Elliot Kaufman was using steroids," Edward said irritated, defensive. "I was concerned that any resultant volatility in his mood might place her in danger."

"What is the exact nature of your relationship with Ms. Meriwether?" Bourke sounded almost bored now.

"I've already answered that question, Detective. Ms. Meriwether and I are friends. We are not involved in any other way."

There were no new questions after that, though the interview continued for another hour. At that point, Ian Denholm became impatient and demanded that the detectives either charge his client or release him. They elected to release him.

Possession

Edward dropped the shopping bags and fell spread-eagled into a bed so tautly made the weight of a grown man barely caused a wrinkle. The superior suite was large, elegantly appointed and, in its particular favour, quite free of blood. His own house was once again a crime scene, being cordoned off, examined, bagged, and labelled—its owner, excluded. The clothes Edward McGinnity had been wearing had been retained by the police. His wallet and the other contents of his pockets, aside from his phone, had been returned to him in a large paper envelope. As a result, he'd been able to purchase some exorbitantly priced polo shirts and jeans at the exclusive arcade in the foyer.

Rousing, Edward rolled off the bed and divested himself of the overalls he'd been given when his clothes were taken as evidence. He showered and shaved using the complimentary hotel toiletry pack before he called Leith Henry.

"No, I'm okay. I'm staying at The Warwick," he said as she exploded with concern and outrage. "You don't need to come, Leith. I'm just going to go to sleep and deal with it in the morning."

He argued with her for a time, assuring her that he was fine, that there was no point in dropping everything and rushing over. She wanted to know details. He promised to recount it all in minutiae the next day.

Edward put down the receiver. It was quiet. Not just audibly, but visually. Surrounded by tasteful, unobtrusive colours, uncommitted décor designed to soothe, he was nevertheless beset by a churning restlessness. Agitated, Edward contemplated seeking some ease of mind in the minibar, before he turned back to take the hotel stationery and pen from the table beside the phone. Everything, it seemed, was going to hell. He'd lost Willow, he couldn't ring Andy, and suddenly his life was full of detectives and violence and allegations. It was not as he would have written it, but then, this was not his doing. He needed to regain some control, a grip on whatever rudder was his to grasp. And so he wrote.

• • ● • •

Madeleine wasn't sure why she told Dr. McCauley about the bloodstained sheets. Perhaps it was just that she needed something to say. Whenever conversation faltered, the psychiatrist only seemed to write more furiously in his notes. It unnerved her. What could he be writing when she wasn't saying anything? And so she kept talking because then at least, she presumed, he'd be writing what she said.

"Why did you not just ask Hugh about the stain?" McCauley posed in response.

"I don't know…" Madeleine already regretted keenly that she'd mentioned it.

"Do you imagine that the stain could be sinister in some way?"

"I'm not sure. He didn't mention it."

"So you feel he's being secretive?"

"I just thought he'd mention it."

McCauley made a note. "Perhaps Hugh was simply embarrassed that he'd soiled the sheets."

"We're talking about blood, not bed-wetting," Madeleine said, exasperated.

"So you make a distinction between bodily fluids?"

"Just blood."

"You seem to be getting a little agitated, Madeleine. Would you say you're feeling anxious?"

"No, I'm not anxious." The psychiatrist was making her anxious but surely that didn't count.

"You write crime fiction, do you not?"

"Yes, but—"

"I wonder if the violent themes you explore in your work are not having an influence here. Do you think that perhaps you are subconsciously turning a mundane mishap into something menacing and suspicious?"

For a moment, Madeleine floundered. "No."

He smiled at her. "If you were completely honest, Madeleine, wouldn't you say that you're responding to this stain as if you were your own hero"—he flicked through his notes—"Edward McGinnity, private eye?"

Madeleine cringed. *Private eye? For God's sake!* "That's insane. No."

McCauley wrote a few notes, his brow furrowing down over his eyes. After a time, he looked up again. "Tell me, are you still having trouble sleeping?"

"No," Madeleine said quickly.

"Hmmm." He looked closely at her face and made one more note.

Madeleine felt a slight flutter of panic. Her father had said she looked tired. Perhaps that's what McCauley saw, too. "I have been working late, but that's because I want to finish this book, not because I can't sleep."

"Insomnia is nothing to be ashamed of, Madeleine. You don't need to make excuses, just to acknowledge and deal with it."

"I'm not—"

"I'd like you to keep a sleep diary, Madeleine. Just write down each day what time you go to bed, when you get up, and what part of that time you actually slept."

"But—"

"I'd really like you to work with me on this, Madeleine. Surely it's not too much to ask for the sake of your health."

Madeleine was beginning to hate McCauley. "Yes, of course. I'll keep a diary."

• • ● • •

Madeleine was cursing by the time she got out to her car. She wiped away enraged tears with her sleeve, frustrated that her fury would choose to express itself this way, that she couldn't stop the collapse, however many calming breaths she took. Madeleine wanted to be haughty, disdainful. She didn't want to cry. McCauley was a smug, condescending bastard! She wasn't going back. She just wouldn't. Who did Hugh think he was insisting she see that sanctimonious buffoon? God, how Edward would hate McCauley. She could see him putting the psychiatrist in his place.

In this thunderous frame, Madeleine pulled into her pebbled driveway, neither surprised nor disappointed that Hugh wasn't home. Throwing her bag at the couch on the way through, she sat on her bed and wept. It was a confused grief, a black choking soup of insult, disenchantment, and fear. She wanted to stamp her foot, to hit back…but at what, she didn't really know.

The laptop sat on her bedside table and Madeleine reached instinctively for it—refuge, the chance to hide in another life. She ran a hand over the aluminium casing, comforted, a gentle easing of the mind, a perceptible slowing of the breath. For a flickering moment she wondered if McCauley was right…was writing her alcohol? Was she anaesthetising herself from her own life? The thought was fleeting, subsumed by a swell of resentment which broke and pounded the memory of McCauley and any possibility of the worth of his counsel.

The bloody sheets played on her mind. They just didn't make sense. As far as she could tell, Hugh had not cut himself. It could have been a nosebleed, she supposed, but why hadn't he mentioned it? And what had he been doing in bed in the middle of the day? Even so, she deeply regretted mentioning the sheets to the psychiatrist. It seemed petty and it was a betrayal of Hugh. Madeleine knew that and she was certain McCauley did too. It frightened her that McCauley was aware of this lapse, this weakness in her marriage and her character.

Madeleine lay back on the bed. Edward lay beside her. She knew that she was daring madness to take her, but right then she cared little. She was defiant now. This was her mind, and she would invite into it anyone she pleased. And Edward McGinnity pleased her. My God, he pleased her.

Edward, too, knew he was courting disaster. But in the anonymous solitude of the hotel room with his own life turning against him, he longed for her company. Not to write, specifically, as much as be with her. He made love to her because he wanted to, regardless of what effect it would have on the story he was crafting for Madeleine d'Leon.

"I could stop thinking about you tomorrow," Madeleine whispered, staring past his shoulder at the ceiling.

"Could you?" he murmured.

"Yes, it's just imagination if you can stop. Delusion has a life of its own."

"I see. Will you stop?"

"I don't want to. I just meant that I could. There's nothing wrong with me."

"Hmmm, but what's wrong with me?"

She trailed her finger idly across his chest. "You? That's easy, you're slumming it in this genre so you can understand the mind of a crime-writer. You literary types go to ridiculous lengths for authenticity."

He laughed. She left her hand on his chest as he did so, embracing the open warmth of his laughter. It was so natural to be with him. There was no chance of misunderstanding…he lived in her head, after all.

"What are you going to do now?" she smiled as she noticed the yellow Vauxhall Cresta on the bedside table.

He kissed her shoulder. "About what?"

"About Willow's allegation."

Edward rolled onto his back and closed his eyes. "I don't know, Maddie. I don't understand why she…" He shook his head.

Madeleine propped herself up on one elbow and gazed at him.

"Do you know?" he asked.

"Not yet. Maybe that's what she thought she saw, Ned. It was all very confused."

"She said I stabbed him!"

"Eyewitness accounts are notoriously unreliable—and not because people are lying."

"I wish I hadn't said anything. I should have known."

Madeleine sat up. His sadness prickled, reminded her that Willow Meriwether was the love she'd written for him. Suddenly she wondered about her own motives.

"Were you surprised?" she asked quietly. "That Willow didn't believe you, that she took Elliot's side? Was it out of character?"

"Not really," he replied. He caught the anxiety in her voice. It intrigued him that she would question her own motives. "Will's always chosen Kaufman. I never understood it until I saw them painting together."

"How do you mean?"

"It was like they were possessed by each other."

"You mean they were in love."

"More than that. They'd forget anybody—anything—else existed. There was only themselves…the work, and the work through themselves, and themselves through the work. They made their own reality. Nothing else could touch it."

Madeleine reached for his hand, interlacing her fingers with his. His grip was warm, strong. Somehow it had substance and force. Some part of her was in wonder that she had conjured this, that she had created such a magnificent delusion. Another part was unsure if she had created him at all.

Edward studied her, mesmerised. How he'd summoned her into being did not bother him enough to contemplate. But he did wonder why. What question was he asking that was answered by Madeleine d'Leon? What was it in his own psyche, his own life that required a crime-writer—was it the death of Geoffrey Vogel? Madeleine had come first, but perhaps he would not have held her so close if it had not been for the events which seemed so suited to her expertise.

Madeleine met his eye and he wondered if she knew what he was thinking. She was probably laughing at him. That was probably fair.

● ● ● ● ●

"Just a minute." Edward tore the swing tag off a polo shirt and pulled it hastily over his head before answering the door. He wasn't expecting anyone, but recent experience had taught him to consider the possibility of the police. If that were so, he did not want to risk being dragged to the station without a shirt. Half-dressed men always looked guilty.

"I say, old man, I hope I'm not intruding." Adrian Barrington radiated courteous goodwill.

"Adrian…no, of course not. Though this is a surprise. How did you know I was here?"

"I was in the station…for Willow, you know. I overheard one of the officers talking about placing men at The Warwick in case you attempted to run." Barrington took a seat in one of the tub-shaped armchairs in the sitting area of the suite.

"Can I make you a cup of coffee, Adrian, or would you prefer something stronger?" Edward asked awkwardly.

"Tea, if you can manage it." The art dealer glanced about the suite as Edward fumbled with teabags and boiling water, visibly cringing at the prints which decorated the wall. He paused when he noticed the bed which showed clear signs of inhabitation. "Oh, I say, you were asleep. I apologise. How rude of me."

Edward placed tea and a couple of UHT milk pods on the table. "I was getting up anyway…please don't be concerned."

Barrington stared at the disarrayed bedclothes. "I see you've tossed and turned. No wonder, of course."

"I've always been a restless sleeper," Edward replied carefully. He could see Madeleine sitting in the bed, watching. "Does Will know you're here, Adrian?"

"Heavens, no! Elliot is not out of the woods, I'm afraid. She's maintaining a vigil at his bedside."

Edward frowned. He decided to be blunt. "Do you mind me asking what you are doing here?"

"Not at all. You're entitled to ask, of course. I was hoping you might tell me exactly what happened."

"Didn't Willow—?"

"Willow is distraught. You may think of us as mere acquaintances, Ned, but I believe I know you rather well. Willow has been talking about you since I first started representing her and we have discussed you often and in great depth. I don't think I'll be betraying a confidence to say she loved you like a brother. I also know Elliot Kaufman. All of this that I know is inconsistent with what Willow says or thinks happened. And so I'm here."

Edward sat back, surprised. "I see. But why do you want to know?"

"I act for Willow. It's easier to do so if I know precisely what's going on."

Edward shrugged. "That seems reasonable, I suppose."

"So will you enlighten me?"

Edward nodded. He told Barrington what had happened: the argument he'd had with Willow, Kaufman's attack, the accident, the blood and his attempts to stop the bleeding.

The art dealer pulled out a green polka-dot silk handkerchief and patted his brow. It was a studied movement. Almost everything about Adrian Barrington seemed designed for effect, without being affected.

"Dear Lord, how appalling!" He took a sip of tea and grimaced his judgment of the brew. "How fortunate that you acted so quickly, Ned!"

"I don't know. Perhaps I should have paused a moment to allow Will to see I hadn't stabbed Kaufman."

"I'll speak to her," Barrington offered. "She'll come round once the shock has passed."

Edward saw Madeleine's eyes narrow. It was enough to make him wary.

"Why?" he asked.

"I beg your pardon?"

"Why do you care how Will feels about me?"

Barrington expanded with an intake of breath and blustered. "Well I…if you…I'm just trying to…" He stood. "I think it's very sad that this experience has made you think the worst of people, Edward! I came here with the very best of intentions. It's really too bad."

Edward retracted, regretting the sharpness of his suspicions. He had no quarrel with Barrington, no reason to distrust him. "I'm sorry, Adrian. I didn't mean to suggest…it's been a difficult day."

Barrington settled somewhat. "Of course, I understand. Perhaps I should not have stuck my oar in."

"No, you were perfectly kind to do so. Anything you might say to Will on my behalf would be greatly appreciated."

Barrington seemed further mollified. He offered Edward his hand. "Say no more, Ned."

Fealty and the Lack Thereof

Peter Blake walked through the open door. Edward McGinnity was sweeping up the last fragments of shattered glass. His sitting room was slowly being put back together.

The reporter whistled. "I thought you'd have someone to do this sort of thing."

Edward smiled. "I fired the butler. I'm afraid Jeeves just wasn't up to the job."

Blake studied him. "So, McGinnity, are you a homicidal maniac or just the unluckiest sap on the planet?"

Edward deposited the glass into a garbage bag. "I'd offer you a seat, but the furniture hasn't been cleaned yet," he said glancing at the couch. The blood splatter was not visible on the dark leather, but it was there. He motioned Blake to follow him into the kitchen instead. Of course it, too, had been a crime scene, but that was weeks ago.

"Thanks." Blake caught the beer that Edward tossed and the two leaned on the breakfast bar to drink and talk. Briefly, Edward recounted what had happened.

"So you saved his life?" Blake said raising his bottle in salute.

Edward shrugged. "Sadly the only other witness is convinced I stabbed him."

"Kaufman?"

"No, he's still sedated. Willow."

"She saw that?"

"She couldn't have—it didn't happen."

Blake set down his beer and took a notebook from his hip pocket. He wrote a couple of notes. "I don't suppose you're willing to consider that Ms. Meriwether may have a less-than-noble reason to accuse you of attempting to murder her husband."

Edward wouldn't have it. "Will was hysterical—mistaken. It wasn't sinister."

Black tapped the pen against his chin, contemplating. "You do know that one of Ms. Meriwether's pieces was sold last week for one hundred and six thousand dollars."

"Really?" Willow had never allowed Edward to buy her paintings and so he had no idea of their market value. "Is that unusual?"

"Let me put it this way, that same painting was bought for fifteen thousand dollars at her exhibition opening."

Edward shrugged. "Her agent did say something about the murder affecting the value. She sold out, you know."

"Well then, some folks have made very astute investments."

"Are you suggesting someone killed Vogel to add value to Will's paintings?" Edward made no effort to hide his scepticism.

"People have been murdered for much less, Eddie boy."

"Still,it seems a little far-fetched—"

"Probably. Why do you think Kaufman attacked you, in the first instance?"

"He probably realised what I was telling Will. Or perhaps he thought he was protecting her somehow. I was trying to make her listen…I grabbed her arm." Edward closed his eyes as he recalled how the nightmare had unfolded. "He came charging in and my bowl of cars was knocked over—"

"Bowl of cars?"

Edward fished the Vauxhall Cresta out of his pocket and showed the reporter.

Blake's face lit up. "Matchbox! Well I'll be buggered—I used to play with these things…always had a couple in my pockets as a kid!"

"I think Kaufman slipped on one of them and fell on the coffee table," Edward said. "Ended up with my fountain pen in his neck."

Blake shook his head. "You wouldn't read about it."

• • ● • •

Hugh closed Madeleine's laptop.

"Hey!" Caught by surprise, Madeleine only just managed to get her hands out of the way.

"Where are the sheets, Maddie?"

"What sheets?"

"Don't pretend you don't know what I'm talking about! We only have one set of white sheets and they're gone!"

"I didn't know you cared so much about the colour of our linen!"

Hugh shouted now. "What the hell did you do with them?"

"Where did the blood come from, Hugh?"

Hugh paled a little, whether from fear or fury, Madeleine could not tell. "What do you think, you idiot? I'm a doctor. I handle blood all the time!"

Madeleine stood folding her arms around the laptop. She held it like a shield before her breast. "It was in our bed, Hugh. What did you do? Dammit! What did you do?"

Silence. It had been said and now there was silence. Loathing and contempt in Hugh Lamond's eyes. Madeleine stepped back, suddenly frightened. He spoke slowly. "I had a vial of blood in my jacket, which I'd forgotten to send off for testing. I lay down for a moment and the vial broke. Blood was spilled. If you had asked me, I would have explained but instead you concoct some wild notion about God-knows-what!"

Madeleine stared at him. Oh God, what had she done? Still. "Whose blood is it, Hugh?"

"Jesus Christ, Maddie, this is not one of your fucking novels! There is no mystery here, just an overworked doctor forgetting to follow protocol with a blood test. Whose blood test it is, is confidential!"

Madeleine felt like he'd slapped her. He looked like he wanted to.

"There's something wrong with you, Maddie!" Hugh had clearly not finished venting his rage. "This is not normal."

"Hugh—"

"I'm going out—to murder people or whatever it is you think I've been doing!"

Madeleine watched as he walked out of the house slamming every door in the process. She felt shaky and wrong-footed. And bereft. She put aside the laptop, angry with herself and with Edward McGinnity.

"You're confusing me," she said bitterly. "You're making me crazy!"

"You believe him, then?" Edward asked.

"What?"

"You believe him about the blood?"

"Why wouldn't I?"

"Only you know that, Maddie."

"Damn you, Ned! It could have happened the way he said!"

He regarded her wordlessly for a time, then he said quietly, "I haven't made you crazy. You are not crazy."

• • ● • •

The shrill ring of the phone startled her. It intruded, and so she was sharp when she answered. It was her father.

"Oh hello, Dad…no, there's nothing wrong. I was just working."

"Ah, I won't bother you then."

"No, it's fine, Dad. I'm always working."

"Asoka Wickramaratne called me about your blood-stain, Madeleine. He's done some tests. He wants you to come to his office."

"His office?" Madeleine groaned. She no longer cared about the blood. "Couldn't I just ring him?"

"I think he has some books he wants you to sign. He buys them all, you know. He must have gone to some trouble to do these tests for you."

Madeleine winced. Clearly, she was going to Asoka Wickramaratne's office. "Yes, of course. I'll go tomorrow—just give me the address."

• • ● • •

Edward had first noticed the SUV, or at least its headlights, several minutes before. The vehicle was a latest model BMW…he assumed the owner had not yet worked out how to switch his lights out of high beam. By the time he reached the outskirts of the city, however, the glare in his rearview and side mirrors was becoming more than a passing annoyance.

He slowed and pulled over to let it pass. And so his car was nearly stationary when the SUV first made impact. Edward cursed and moved to get out of his vehicle, expecting that the other driver would do the same. As he swung open the door, the SUV reversed and gunned its engine once again. Edward hesitated, and then he heard Madeleine scream, "Now, Ned, go now!"

He turned the ignition and slammed the accelerator to the floor before he'd even closed the door.

The BMW corrected too late, slid past the Jag's rear bumper, braked hard and turned in pursuit.

On the road, Edward wasn't sure what to do. It seemed he had somehow become involved in a car chase. The Mark II was not accustomed to being driven hard— he was not sure she was up to anything this strenuous, not to mention insane—he was not sure he was up to it either. The SUV was trying to pass him in order to cut him off or run him off the road again. He turned hard into a bend, hearing the squeal of tyres behind as the SUV fishtailed before regaining control. Edward had no idea where he was going, just away.

"Drive back towards the city," Madeleine instructed.

"Why?"

"Traffic, witnesses—she's got a clear run here, nothing but road and no one to see."

"Are you crazy, Maddie? He's driving like a lunatic. If there's traffic someone will get killed!"

"She's chasing you down, Ned. You are going to get killed! You have to go towards help!"

Edward's eyes flashed, the lines of his jaw became hard. "I will not be the cause of a car accident!"

Madeleine pulled back. Of course. He wouldn't. What had she been thinking? "Then you'll have to lose them. How fast is this thing?"

"She's pretty swift in short bursts, but she's an old car, Maddie."

"We'll have to hide."

"What?"

"Go as fast you can. When you lose sight of the BMW on a bend or over the crest of a hill, pull off the road and kill the engine. With any luck they'll drive past."

"Do you think that will work?" he asked sceptically.

"It does in my books."

Despite his misgivings, Edward did as she instructed, opening up the throttle. The burst of speed caught the SUV by surprise. Edward smiled grimly as the force of the acceleration threw him back into the leather seat and the headlights in his rearview mirror receded rapidly. He wasn't sure how much of a lead he'd clawed by the time he pulled off into a small laneway which offered a screening of trees. He could not bring himself to drive the Jaguar completely off road.

Madeleine watched Edward McGinnity grimace as he cut the engine.

"Living might be just slightly more important than allowing the engine to cool," she whispered.

Edward did not seem entirely convinced.

Seconds passed, and then a minute. A car sped past, but from his position behind the trees, Edward could not see if it was the SUV. Madeleine did not allow him to lose time wondering. "Go, now!"

He turned the key. For a few spluttering moments the car resisted and Madeleine feared that all Hugh's warnings about the importance of allowing the engine to cool were warranted, after all. Then, finally, the engine ignited. Edward pointed his car in the direction from which he had come and once again pressed the accelerator pedal to the floor.

Madeleine was struggling to understand the twisting of her own mind. She wasn't really sure what she was putting into train or why. She had no idea who was trying to run Edward McGinnity off the road. Elliot Kaufman was in hospital…Adrian Barrington, perhaps…or Willow?…She shook her head to dislodge the thought. Willow Meriwether was one of the good guys, her hero's love interest…not that Edward really loved Willow…he'd just thought he did.

She manoeuvred her old Mercedes into the tight parking space, wondering, not for the first time whether she should sacrifice the classic style of her vintage automobile for the convenience of power steering. She climbed out feeling like she'd heaved the car into place. Still, she was lucky to have found a space at all at this time of day.

Dr. Asoka Wickramaratne worked on the twenty-seventh floor of the building adjacent to the car park. The forensic pathologist, a solid gentleman, as wide as he was tall, moved and spoke with a kind of measured caution.

"Hello, Uncle," Madeleine said as she walked into his office. An extraordinarily small skull leered up at her from the desk. A child's skull, perhaps. The thought hurt. The callous disrespect of the poor wee thing's resting place on the pathologist's desk was distressing.

"It's a pencil sharpener," Wickramaratne said, picking it up to show her the mechanism embedded in the bottom. "My son's idea of a joke."

Madeleine nodded, relieved but hoping she didn't look so.

They small-talked for a while—about her father, curry recipes, and of course the cricket. Of the latter two subjects, Madeleine knew little, but Wickramaratne's enthusiasm more than compensated.

Eventually, Madeleine was able to raise the matter for which she had come.

"Oh, yes, your blood sample. What would you like to know, Madeleine?"

Madeleine hesitated. She should tell Wickramaratne that she already knew where the blood came from, but she didn't, waiting instead for him to tell her.

"The blood type is B negative. The source is a female."

"Female?"

"There were uterine cells present. The blood is menstrual."

"Menstrual?" Madeleine swallowed as agony caught in her throat.

"Yes, yes." His head bobbed vigorously up and down. "It's unlikely the stain was the result of some kind of violence. There's nothing untoward about it at all."

"On the face of it." Madeleine forced a smile. It was an effort.

"Yes, yes, prima facie. In your hands, I'm sure it will be much more interesting." Wickramaratne returned the sheet to her in a plastic bag, and had her sign her books while he speculated about how she would use the information he had given her. He didn't once ask where the sheet had come from and why it was important. Madeleine was grateful, but she did wonder what he actually thought crime-writers did.

She got through pleasantries, thanked her father's friend for his help and left him to his real work.

Back in the car, Madeleine sat. She felt over-aware—her impulse to shut down, to close her eyes and cover her ears and retreat. She didn't want to start thinking because she knew what conclusions awaited her there. She didn't want to know that for a while.

"Maddie," Edward whispered. "I'm sorry."

"Shhhh." Madeleine could feel his arms around her and that was all she could take at that moment. She just wanted to rest her head on Edward's shoulder and not think about Hugh. Minutes of nothing became hours. Occasionally a passing Samaritan would tap on the window and ask if she was okay. She'd respond with a nod, a tentative wave, or say she was waiting for her husband.

And then Madeleine let the thought through.

She was O positive. The blood in her bed could not have been hers. There had been another woman in her bed and Hugh had lied about it. She rested her head on the steering wheel, fighting waves of nausea and fury. And through all of this, Edward McGinnity held her and in doing so reminded her that he was there, and that he had made love to her in that bed.

"You're different," she wept. "You're not real."

Flight

Edward turned off the headlights and allowed the car to idle for a few minutes. He rested his head on the steering wheel wondering for a moment if he had imagined the SUV. He climbed out and walked around behind the vehicle. The back light cover was smashed and the rear bumper badly dented. He hadn't imagined it completely. But the pursuit...he'd not seen the SUV again after doubling back. Was he allowing the stress to get to him?

He let himself into the house, disarming the security system as he did so. The living room had not yet been returned to order after Elliot Kaufman's accident and the subsequent police investigation. Edward hadn't had the time to restore the contents of his bookshelves which sat in piles on the sideboard. He'd cleaned up the broken glass, but the collection of Matchbox cars had not been returned. The yellow Vauxhall Cresta was in his pocket and he touched it now like some kind of talisman—warding off what, he did not know.

Edward was caught by a sudden feeling that he did not want to be here, that he wished to be anywhere but here. The decision to go came soon thereafter. A change of scene. Someplace quiet where he could write, where he could clear space in his head, someplace he could explore Madeleine without distraction. He ran up to the bedroom and pulled a duffel bag from beneath a pile of running shoes and tennis racquets in the cupboard. He stuffed it with enough clothes for a few days as well as his notebooks. He glanced up at the nude on his wall, the painted muse who had seen him through all the struggles of his craft in the past. "This is not good-bye," he said smiling at her. "I just need to untangle some things and then I'll be back. I promise."

He considered for a moment whether he should ring Denholm or Leith to tell them of his plans, such as they were. A call when he got there would suffice, he decided. At the moment he had no idea where he was going to end up.

Edward was reminded of the damage to his car when he threw his bag into the boot. Still, it was on the whole cosmetic...he'd worry about repairs later once he'd found a place where he could write.

"Are you running away?" Madeleine whispered.

He started the car. "From what, Maddie?"

"I'm not sure...the police, I guess."

He laughed. "They'll never take me alive!" he said. "Come on, Maddie, we're both better than that."

"Better what?"

He paused. "Writers," he said finally. He pulled his phone from his pocket. "I'll be perfectly contactable— all they have to do is ring."

Madeleine nodded. "Okay."

"What about you?" he asked tilting his head. "Are you ever going to get out of this car and confront Hugh?"

Madeleine frowned. She could see the house and Hugh's car in the driveway from where she sat parked across the road. It was drizzling and misty and the house looked cosy and quaint, like it belonged on the lid of a tin of shortbread. The young greens in the garden seemed to glow in this light. Her house, her garden. It was all about to change. The moment she walked into that house there would be no going back. There was already no going back.

And yet some part of her resisted, clung, bargained. Madeleine wondered what would happen if she said nothing. Would Hugh return to her? Would he give up the woman with B negative blood? Could they put it behind them as they had the miscarriages? What if she never told him that she knew? Madeleine closed her eyes…she was so confused, so angry and hurt.

For a time she sat, having imaginary conversations with Hugh and with B negative woman. She rehearsed righteous fury, vengefulness, dignified indifference. And Edward watched her. Eventually she drove the Mercedes through the gate, and walked into her house.

Hugh Lamond looked up from the sink.

"Hello, Maddie. Where have you been?"

Madeleine hesitated. This was the moment. The moment in which she would decide the rest of her life.

Hugh dried up a second wineglass and she decided. "I had an appointment with a forensic pathologist."

"Research?" he asked already losing interest.

"No." She extracted the plastic envelope containing the bloodstained sheet from her bag. Her hand was shaking. She was scared…not of Hugh, but scared.

Hugh's face became dark and hard. He glanced at the envelope, but the full fury of his scrutiny he reserved for Madeleine.

"Don't be frightened," Edward said as he saw her waver, panic. "I'm here with you."

She calmed. "This blood wasn't drawn, Hugh. It wasn't in a vial."

"No. It wasn't."

Madeleine faltered. She hadn't been prepared for so blatant an admission. She was not sure what to say next. "What...who...whose blood is it?"

"Do you really want to know? Or have you come with a story that will suit you better?"

"Just tell me!" Madeleine was shouting now.

"It's a patient's."

"You're sleeping with one of your patients?"

Hugh moved towards her and then stepped back as if restraint required him to keep some distance. His nostrils flared as he exhaled. "I wasn't sleeping with her. She was lying down while I called an ambulance."

"What was she doing here, Hugh?"

"She's a maternity patient. She came to the house because she started to cramp and panicked and, like every other person in town, she knows where I live. I realised she was probably miscarrying and told her to lay down while I called an ambulance."

"In our bedroom?" Madeleine was incredulous... how stupid did he think she was?

"She needed to use the bathroom. I told her to use our en suite because nobody's cleaned the other one in weeks! She became lightheaded when she came out and our bed was the nearest." Hugh's voice was just slightly unsteady.

"Then why did you tell me you'd broken a vial of blood?" Madeleine demanded with just a note of touché.

"Because the patient is a sixteen-year-old girl who wanted and is entitled to privacy!"

"I'm your wife, Hugh! You're talking about something which supposedly happened in our bed!"

"Yes, you're my wife!" Hugh shouted back now. "Why don't you act like it? Why don't you trust me instead of running around like some demented Mata Hari?"

"How dare you!" Madeleine couldn't contain her fury. It pumped through every artery and vein, seized every organ with a kind of crazed outrage. "You deceived me! Don't make it sound like it's my fault!"

"I told one lie, to respect a patient's privacy and because the subject of miscarriage is not one you can handle with any degree of reason." Hugh's voice lowered dangerously. "And you respond by calling in the bloody CSI! It's not normal, Maddie!"

Madeleine wanted to hit him. Curse at him. She wiped her nose with her sleeve. When had she started crying? She did not know. Perhaps weeks ago.

"You can't see how delusional you've become, can you, Maddie? You always had so much going on in your head...I loved that about you...but you've let it take over. You can't tell the difference between what's real and what you've made up. Don't think I haven't seen you talking to yourself or, worse still, to him!"

Madeleine stepped back now. "That's just—" she began.

"Where you'd prefer to be!" Hugh spat. "With him

and all your other made-up people, solving imaginary murders! You're sick, Maddie. You can't see it but I can."

"Trust me, I'm a doctor," Madeleine said coldly. "Only I can't trust you, can I, Hugh? You lie to me when it suits you and you expect me to believe the second lie when the first is revealed!"

Hugh sighed. He regarded his wife silently for a moment. "Darling, I think you're having a breakdown of some sort. It's no wonder, after what you've been through."

"What I've been through?"

"The miscarriages."

"You went through that, too, Hugh. Perhaps you're the one having the breakdown. Some kind of midlife crisis complete with a mistress!"

"You're wrong, Maddie."

Madeleine shook her head. "I don't want to talk to you anymore." She grabbed her bag from the table. "I have work to do."

She went into their bedroom only to grab pyjamas from the lowboy and shut herself in the spare room. It didn't have a bed but the retired couch was large enough to sleep on. There was an old quilt in the blanket box which doubled as a coffee table. With it wrapped around her Madeleine retreated, shrinking into the worn cushions. She felt like she was drowning and yet she had an overwhelming urge to let go of the side.

"Are you running now?" Edward asked.

"I'm not going anywhere."

"But you are running."

"Hugh might be telling the truth."

"About what, exactly?"

"The patient...the blood."

"If you were writing this story, Maddie, would he be telling the truth?"

"This is my life, not a story," Madeleine replied uncertainly. "Real life is full of coincidences and scenarios too far-fetched for fiction."

"It's also full of liars. In fiction the only liar is the author himself."

Madeleine groaned. "What does that mean?"

Edward smiled. He loved her lack of pretension. "When you write you know who the liars are, or at least who they could be. In real life, liars are—" he searched for the word, "unexpected."

"You're thinking about Willow?"

"Not just about Willow. But, yes, Willow."

"She surprised me too," Madeleine said quietly. But she wondered. Was it Willow Meriwether's actions or her own that surprised her? Madeleine was aware that she no longer wanted Edward to love Willow. Was that behind Willow's betrayal? And then, deep in her gut, a sour thought fermented: *Was Hugh right?*

A knock on the door. "Maddie?"

Madeleine said nothing.

The door opened. Hugh stood silhouetted against the bright light of the hallway. He held a steaming mug and plate of buttered toast. "You didn't eat. I brought you a cup of tea." He smiled slightly, tentatively. "Jeeves' night off, you know."

Madeleine might have thanked him if she hadn't been crying already.

Hugh set the plate and mug down on the blanket box. He squatted beside the couch without making a move to touch his weeping wife. "Maddie, how about you go see Dr. McCauley tomorrow? Just talk it over with him. It might help."

Madeleine tried to pull herself together.

Hugh rubbed his face. "I hate to see you so unhappy, Darling. I know you're angry with me at the moment but—" He shook his head. "Let's not go into all that again, for now anyway. Can't you just see McCauley one more time? If it doesn't help, we'll try something else. But, Maddie, we just can't go on like this." He picked up the tea and held it out to her.

Madeleine took it and pressed the mug against her lips. The warmth of it was calming. Against the china her lips stopped trembling. She nodded. "Okay," she said hoarsely, her eyes fixed on the tea.

Still he didn't try to touch her. Madeleine was honestly not sure if she wanted him to, and yet she felt strangely disappointed, rejected.

"I'll call him," he said standing. "Try to get some sleep. Hopefully, it won't seem so bleak in the morning."

The light narrowed and disappeared as he closed the door behind him. In the darkness, Madeleine remained. The confusion churned. Her leg moved restlessly, like she was bouncing an invisible child on her knee, and her fingers tapped an agitated accelerating rhythm until finally she allowed them to reach for the laptop.

Tomorrow she would deal with the tawdry machinations of life, the negotiations, the practicalities, the reasoning. She would see Dr. McCauley. She would be objective, and rational, and sane. But tonight...tonight she would escape with Edward McGinnity

Return

The docks were well-maintained, recently painted and colour-coordinated. The boats moored here were polished indulgent vessels of gleaming timbers and burnished chrome—pleasure craft which left the café-lined port only occasionally when conditions on the bay were perfect. They waited like tethered swans for release on the warmer days when the wind did not cut so bitterly over the water.

Edward grabbed his duffel bag from the boot. The docks were empty of life but for an old man drinking on the deck of the yacht in the second mooring. *The Lady Galadriel* was, if he remembered correctly, moored a little further up the wharf. Andy Finlay had purchased the boat from a client some years ago. He'd taken Edward out on it occasionally and entrusted his ward with the knowledge of where the spare key was hidden.

It had been a cheap ship-in-a-bottle on display at the service station where he'd stopped to refuel that made Edward think of *The Lady Galadriel*. By then, it was late so he had driven straight to the dock, resolving to call Finlay the following morning for permission to stay on the boat.

The key was where he'd expected, taped to the lid of the box which contained the spare life jackets. The cabin smelled fresh—recently cleaned. Edward supposed that there was a regular maintenance and cleaning crew who kept the boat seaworthy or at least worthy of mooring at this address. He couldn't remember Andy Finlay mentioning the boat in years; he doubted the lawyer had set foot aboard in quite some time.

The cabin was large, with separate living and dining areas and two bedrooms below. The refrigerator was empty but Edward had purchased milk and a packet of chocolate biscuits at the service station. There was coffee in the cupboard. That would do him for a while.

Edward set his notebook and fountain pen on the coffee table and tossed a few cushions off the couch to make room for himself. The cabin was cool, not uncomfortably so but enough to make him aware of the air on his skin. He couldn't remember if he needed to run the engine to use the heating so he left it, rummaging through his duffel bag to find a pullover instead.

He was looking forward to returning to Madeleine, though in truth he'd been with her for some time. She was always there beside him now, to talk to, to make love to, but her story was more than that. The narrative was poised. Madeleine had been confronted with truth and betrayal. All that remained was what she would do. Edward toyed with the idea of the end. He felt changed by Madeleine d'Leon, but perhaps that was as it should be. Perhaps that was the secret of genesis. He could hear her laughing at that thought.

"It's just a story, Ned...not the Bible."

He picked up his pen, admiring her simple belief in story for its own sake, without the self-consciousness of saying something more than what happened. Perhaps that's what he was seeking through her, the purity of story without the shackles of secondary meaning.

Again he could see her rolling her eyes.

He smiled and began to write.

• • ● • •

Madeleine tried to mask the darkness under her eyes with a lighter foundation, but the result just made her look pale. For a moment she contemplated whether eyeliner would disguise or enhance the redness. Concluding the latter, she left her eyes alone.

Hugh had made her appointment with McCauley for ten. And he'd been kind that morning, bringing her tea and then ducking into town for fresh croissants and brioche. And yet she wanted to be angry with Hugh. Madeleine feared she would lose herself if she could not hang on to that anger. She'd rung Leith when her husband departed for the bakery.

"If I leave now, I can be there in a couple of hours, Maddie," Leith said.

"I can't bring my agent to see my psychiatrist."

"Why not? I'm a psychologist!"

"I don't think Dr. McCauley will care." Madeleine hesitated before she asked, "Leith, do you think I'm—"

"Mad? No." Leith's voice softened. "I do think that you've been working very intensely, that this new book has taken a lot out of you. But you're a writer…that shouldn't be a surprise. It's what you do."

"What about Hugh? The blood…?"

"To be honest, Maddie, bringing in a forensic special-ist is probably a bit unusual, but that might be because not everyone's father knows one."

"But do you think—?"

Leith was silent for a few seconds. "I don't know, Maddie. Hugh's story sounds plausible but you're in a better position to know if he's lying. You live in a small country town—would he be able to hide an affair?"

"I haven't really been into town much since I started writing Edward. I haven't talked to anyone here for a while." Madeleine remembered Lilian saying weeks ago that she was neglecting Hugh...that there were women would give anything to be married to Hugh Lamond. Was that a warning? Should she have paid more attention?

"Are you sure you don't want me to come?" Leith asked.

"No. I'm fine, just tired. I'll call you after I speak to McCauley. I might need a second opinion." Madeleine took Edward McGinnity's hand as she hung up the phone. She wasn't afraid of Gerry McCauley.

Hugh drove her to McCauley's consulting rooms himself. He didn't come in. Madeleine didn't pause to consider how she would get home. She assumed Hugh would wait. That was a good sign, she supposed, that he was willing to wait for her.

The psychiatrist asked her to go in while he had a brief word with his secretary. Madeleine took the armchair closer to the door this time. McCauley was not long. He walked in with an open file in his hand, looking up to nod at her just before he sat down. "Good morning, Madeleine. I'm so glad you decided to come in."

Edward stood by the desk behind McCauley, his arms folded. Madeleine smiled at him. McCauley accepted it. He started by asking after her writing, flicking back in his notes for specifics. She answered warily. "My publishers wish to see the finished manuscript next week," she said in the end. Having the manuscript wanted by publishers, giving it a deadline, seemed to give it some external respectability—a commercial reality and with it a justification of her commitment, her immersion.

"And has your hero…Edward, isn't it? Has he solved the murder of this chap Vogel, yet?"

"No. I haven't really decided who did it yet."

McCauley displayed surprise and interest. "Oh, I'd always assumed mystery writers knew that sort of thing from the beginning."

"Some do, but I don't really plot. Not consciously, anyway. For a while there I thought Adrian Barrington would be the murderer."

"Barrington!" Edward said sceptically.

"The murder was financially lucrative for him… the 'macabre provenance' he spoke of. And Geoffrey Vogel's negative review, if published, would have had the opposite effect."

"But the blood in my en suite," Edward said, moving away from the desk and sitting instead on McCauley's consulting couch.

"I wondered if he'd sent in men to plant evidence in the house of Edward McGinnity," Madeleine replied. "The assault was designed to ensure the police would search the house as a crime scene and find the blood in the en suite."

"But you don't intend this character, Barrington, to be the culprit anymore?" McCauley prompted.

"I don't think he did it anymore."

"Then who?" McCauley leant forward, regarding her intently.

Madeleine glanced at Edward. How could she tell him about Willow…his best friend, the woman he had loved for so long, her rival…"In the end I suppose the author is always the murderer," she said. "We decide who'll live, who'll die and why. In the end, it's us."

"Do you like that, Madeleine, deciding questions of life and death, having the power to take or give such things?" McCauley pressed.

Madeleine shrugged. The conversation was taking an uncomfortably existentialist turn. "I like being a writer."

McCauley nodded. "If you don't mind my saying, Madeleine, you look tired. Did you sleep much last night?"

"Well, no," Madeleine admitted. "I was working on—"

"Do you ever worry that fatigue may be detrimental to your writing?"

"Well, not as such—"

"Sleep is one of those things, Madeleine. You don't sleep, so you're tired, so you become fatigued and a little emotional. Things seem more insurmountable than they would otherwise, so you begin to doubt yourself, and with that worry comes wakefulness and so the cycle repeats."

"I'm not sure what you're saying, Dr. McCauley."

"I'm suggesting that we could address a lot of your current problems by simply ensuring you got a good night's sleep."

"Oh." Madeleine stopped, surprised. McCauley seemed to have finally accepted there was nothing wrong with her. She was just tired. Perhaps she had misjudged the psychiatrist.

"What I'd like to do, Madeleine, is sort out your sleeping problem."

"Oh…yes. That sounds like a good idea…"

"We'd need to observe some of your sleep patterns, monitor you. It means we'll need to admit you to the hospital, as a voluntary patient."

"I don't have the time."

"You could bring your work with you…I'll organise a private room. We'll just need to monitor you for about seventy-two hours, and then we'll be able to figure out exactly how to ensure you're getting the sleep you require to function with the clarity a writer needs."

Madeleine looked at Edward. She could see the question in his eyes. Did he doubt her motives?…Did he suspect that she was sacrificing the integrity of her narrative for him, recasting her villain to remove the woman he'd loved? Was that what she was doing? Had she decided to eliminate Willow from Edward's heart to make way for herself? Perhaps McCauley was right… she needed to find some clarity. She was too close, too tired. "What would I have to do?"

McCauley nodded, smiling in a display of reassurance. "Not a great deal. I have rounds at the hospital so I could take you myself. I'll ring Hugh and tell him to meet us there. We fill in some paperwork and you take a little vacation in a private room while we monitor you." He glanced at the satchel at her feet. "Is that your laptop?"

"Yes."

"Good. You'll have work with you, then. I'll just tell Hugh to bring you some pyjamas and toiletries, unless there's anything else you'd like?"

"No…" Madeleine said, a little bewildered by how quickly his suggestion had become organised into an agreed course. But perhaps that was because she'd been so indecisive of late. Three days in a hospital, to stop life and just write. In that time, she could finish the novel… think about a sequel…a series. At the end of it, they would give her some sleeping pills, which she could use or not…but three days with nothing to think about but Edward McGinnity.

She waited while McCauley made some phone calls and when he returned, she signed the admission papers he brought her. Edward remained. As time passed, Madeleine became settled with the idea of a recuperative retreat, and her mind began to drift to Edward's story even as McCauley drove her to the St Aiden's Private Hospital. She didn't pay any significant attention to the admission procedures, or to Hugh when he arrived with her necessities. He approved, of course, promised that he and Jeeves would take care of things till she got home. Madeleine was relieved when she was finally shown to a room and allowed to open her laptop.

Edward put down his pen. He pressed the heels of his palms into his eyes. He felt sick. He wanted to warn her, to protect her. But he wanted to write her story… he couldn't flinch now.

He watched as Madeleine chewed her bottom lip as she stared at the screen. Twice she started to type and backspaced.

"What's wrong?" Edward asked, curious. He'd become accustomed to the certainty with which she wrote.

She swallowed, gathering courage. This was her story; her choice whatever her reasons. "It's Willow," she said. "Willow killed Geoffrey Vogel."

"That doesn't make sense," he replied, shaking his head. "She was with me."

"When his body was found, not when he was killed."

"Even so, she was fine, worried about finding a joke for her speech, for God's sake! How could she have just killed a man?"

For a moment Madeleine faltered, struggled. She clutched at Willow's nervousness to find a foreshadowing. "Perhaps it wasn't the speech that was unsettling her; perhaps it was the fact that she'd pushed a man down the stairs."

"That's thin, Maddie, and you know it. You're a better writer than this."

Madeleine flinched, but she set her mind. "It's what happened."

Still he tried to reason with her. "Willow helped me get the security footage and she definitely didn't beat me up."

Madeleine fought. "Of course she did. She knew there was nothing on the footage—the security guard had already shown her. And Elliot organised his mates from the gym to attack you…and to plant Vogel's blood. It must have been them in the SUV that tried to run you off the road."

"Why would Kaufman do that?"

"Because he loves Willow and he knows that she did it."

"Maddie, be sensible. Where would Kaufman get Vogel's blood?"

"He was there, remember? Watching Willow. Maybe he found the body first. Perhaps he got blood on himself then, and later used it to implicate you."

Edward shook his head. "No. Will wouldn't..."

"She did. She might not have intended for suspicion to fall on you, she might not have intended to kill Vogel, but she knows it wasn't you...she must know."

Edward's voice became strained. He stood and paced. "Willow's been my best friend for years, Maddie. She didn't do this. You're wrong."

"She said you stabbed Elliot. Ned, it fits. Why else would she lie? It's not obvious, but it makes sense."

"Not to me," he said. "You can't think this, you can't."

There was a gentle knock on the door. "Maddie?" Hugh Lamond peered into the room. "You're still awake."

She nodded. "It's only just past ten."

"You're here to get some rest."

"I've been lying about all day. If I was any more rested, I'd be dead."

Hugh pulled up a chair beside the bed. "You're supposed to be getting some sleep." He tapped the cover of her laptop. "Perhaps you should turn this off for a while. Concentrate on getting better."

Madeleine glanced at Edward. He shook his head. She closed the computer.

Hugh smiled. "I feel like that screen's been between us for weeks."

"That's not what's come between us, Hugh."

He sighed. "No, I guess it isn't. You stopped trusting me."

"You started lying to me."

"Oh, Maddie. You were fragile. I was trying not to upset you."

"Fragile?" Madeleine could feel her body tensing to recoil.

Hugh spoke calmly. "Darling, I know you want to pretend you're fine, that you're not sad, but it's just not true. You've been struggling for a while."

"Struggling with what?"

"With reality. I don't blame you for not wanting to deal with the miscarriages—for retreating into that wonderful, crazy, brilliant imagination of yours. Infertility is a difficult thing to accept."

"I'm not infertile." An old panic clutched cold at her breast. "You don't know that I'm infertile."

"Dammit, Maddie! Despite everything that's happened, you won't even consider the possibility, let alone talk about it. You'd rather talk about God-knows-what with some bloke you made up."

"I'm not crazy, either, Hugh, or depressed, or whatever else you want to diagnose me with to salve your own conscience."

"I'm not trying to salve anything, Maddie. Darlin', can't you bring yourself to admit that he isn't real?"

"I'm not the one that needs to admit to anything!" Madeleine brushed the tears away with the sleeve of her pyjamas.

Hugh's face softened. "Maddie, even if I were having an affair, don't you see that retreating into an imaginary world is not a normal or healthy way to deal with it?"

"Hugh, I'm a writer. Stories are how I understand the world."

"You're using stories to hide from the world, Maddie. You have to stop."

"You want me to stop writing?"

"I think—no, I know—it's the only way you'll get better. For all our sakes, you have to."

For a moment Madeleine simply stared. Hugh's face seemed less familiar somehow. His eyes were different. She looked into them, searching, and then her gaze moved past him.

Edward reached for her. "I love you, Maddie." He made the declaration impulsively, almost as surprised by the sound of the words as by the truth of them.

She turned away from him and spoke to her husband. "I can't. I can't stop."

The cabin lights dimmed. Edward looked up. A red warning light had come on above the door—the batteries were low. He cursed, pulling away from his thoughts, from Madeleine, to address the impending darkness. He couldn't write without light.

It had been about five years since Edward had last spent any time on *The Lady Galadriel.* Andy Finlay had been hosting some international clients and so Edward had overseen the day-to-day practicalities of pleasure cruising whilst his lawyer drank champagne, ate seafood, and secured several million dollars in business. Edward vaguely recalled that the engine needed to be run to recharge the batteries.

He stepped out onto the deck and scanned the boats alongside for signs of habitation. They were both completely dark. He decided to risk the less-than-considerate or neighbourly action of running the engine on idle at that hour.

The lights brightened immediately as the engines turned over. Edward's face relaxed as the motor settled into a familiar throb. Perhaps he'd take *Galadriel* out when life had calmed down and he was able to think of normal things again. It was possibly the hum of the engine that masked the noise and left him oblivious until the door to the cabin was forced.

Edward wasn't sure why he fought. Perhaps it was instinct or some memory of the last attack. He didn't pause to register the police uniform, he didn't hear the shouted identification. He felled the first officer with a punch but the second and third brought him down, slamming him bodily to the timber floor. The salty metallic taste of blood in his mouth. The air pounded out of his lungs. His hands were cuffed behind his back whilst he was pinned with a knee against his spine. Then Bourke was there to make the arrest.

"You weren't thinking of leaving were you, McGinnity?"

"I was just recharging the batteries."

But Bourke had made up his mind that this was some attempt to flee by boat. Edward's passport was discovered in the zippered pocket of his duffel bag. He tried to explain that he'd not taken it out after returning from a holiday in London months ago, that he'd simply forgotten it was there.

Bourke was uninterested. He informed Edward that Elliot Kaufman had regained consciousness to support his wife's version of events. That the security footage had not picked up enough to clear him or contradict the witnesses' accounts. Edward McGinnity was being charged with the attempted murder of Kaufman and the murder of Geoffrey Vogel, as well as the attempted theft of *The Lady Galadriel*. "I'd like to see your fancy brief get you out this time," Bourke snarled once Edward had been read his rights.

Madeleine typed steadily. This was it—the point of despair, when the protagonist was faced with annihilation, when he showed his mettle by fighting on. The natural structure of crime fiction; it was comforting to find it. This was what she knew. As much as all seemed lost now, Edward would prevail, Madeleine would write him out of destruction.

She glanced at the clock. Hugh would be here soon to pick her up. Madeleine had decided to go home early. There was nothing wrong with her. Dr. McCauley had talked her into this when the knowledge of Hugh's betrayal was still so new that she would do anything to deny it, as Edward had denied Willow's. But she knew now. As much as the realisation made her feel flayed, as much as every nerve screamed with the agony of it, she knew. She was not mad, just in pain and wiser.

Hugh Lamond came in with McCauley.

"Hello," Madeleine smiled brightly, so there was no question of depression. She gestured towards the small bag on her bed. "I'm ready."

"I had hoped you'd agree to stay a little longer, Madeleine."

"I really must get home, Dr. McCauley. I'm fine now, and I slept very well last night."

"Hugh and I have been discussing your progress, Madeleine," McCauley said evenly. "We've decided it would be in your best interests to stay here for a little while, until we can address some of your problems."

"What problems?" Madeleine asked, startled.

"You talk to imaginary people, Maddie," Hugh replied. "You're imagining murders and conspiracies and God-knows-what! And you don't even want to stop."

"I'm imagining it, am I, Hugh?" Madeleine came back angrily. "Is that what you're telling yourself?"

McCauley put up his hand to caution Hugh. "Madeleine, it concerns me that you are speaking of doing violence, that you see yourself as an arbitrator of life and death."

"As a writer, you idiot!" Madeleine spat. "Well, I'm not staying!" She grabbed the laptop. "You can both go to hell!"

"I'm afraid I can't sign your release papers while I hold these concerns, Madeleine." McCauley stood his ground.

"Sign, don't sign. I don't care," Madeleine said attempting to sidestep him. "I'm going."

McCauley moved out of the way. Two male health workers stood in the doorway. "I'm afraid you can't, Madeleine. Hugh and I both agree that you should remain here for your own good."

Madeleine stared at the men who barred her way, realising suddenly that Hugh and McCauley were trying to commit her. Horror. Fury. Fear. She charged the health workers in a desperate attempt to run. To get out of the hospital.

"Maddie…"

She could hear Hugh pleading with her.

The health workers seized her. Madeleine struggled. The laptop slipped from her hands, falling open as it hit the floor. The screen shattered and the hard plastic shell of the computer cracked. Madeleine screamed, striking out at her captors as she scrambled to retrieve it. What followed was blurred with tears and panic. The humiliation of a strait jacket and sedatives. Hugh turned his back and she was confined. And she screamed for Edward. Wept for Edward who waited in prison for her to write him out.

Edward didn't write, couldn't write. His notebooks had been taken as evidence that first night. Leith and Denholm had done their best, but with two witnesses who swore he'd stabbed Elliot Kaufman, things did not go well. Denholm lodged an appeal as soon as the verdict was handed down. Peter Blake had secured a book deal with Middleton Meyer. The purportedly intimate portrait of Edward McGinnity, orphan, celebrated novelist, and vicious murderer was expected to be a bestseller. Edward's own sales figures had also soared. Leith brought him clippings of the reviews which invariably detected homicidal predilections in his work.

The penitentiary felt strangely familiar, an adult version of the boys' home to which he'd been consigned for a time years ago, when, after escaping from the foster home for a third time, it had been decided that he was uncontrollable. Paper and pencils were a privilege which he would have to earn with good behaviour, compliance which required a deadening of the spirit and the mind. Instead Edward retreated. Some part of him had broken with the realisation that it was Willow who had betrayed him from the first. He grieved the friendship but nothing else. He didn't want to finish his manuscript; he was not sure why. For a while Madeleine d'Leon's story had been everything, but now he wanted only to keep her to himself. He couldn't expose her to the scrutiny of the world. He didn't have that courage anymore.

They wouldn't allow Madeleine to write in the hospital. Her laptop was beyond repair anyway, and her manuscript lost. Hugh sold the television rights to the Veronica Killwilly novels with the power of attorney Madeleine had granted him. The series was a ratings and commercial success, and film and merchandising deals were quick to follow. In all of this, Madeleine had no interest. But she watched Edward still, thought about him, dreamt about him. By forbidding her to write, they'd given her permission just to be with him undistracted by plots or twists or inconvenient love interests. Now he was simply hers.

"Maddie, darling, what can I do?"

She looked past the doctors, the orderlies, and smiled at him.

McCauley couldn't explain Madeleine d'Leon's decline. He could not diagnose what caused her increasing detachment from reality, her lack of interest in getting better. Hugh visited once or twice and then he stopped. Madeleine barely noticed.

• • ● • •

IN THE END, he was a thought so whole that she was aware of nothing else.

To see more Poisoned Pen Press titles:

Visit our website:
poisonedpenpress.com/
Request a digital catalog:
info@poisonedpenpress.com